TATTOOTIE

Jo Hammers

Paranormal Crossroads & Publishing

Tattootie

Copyright © 2011 by Jo Hammers

ISBN 978-0-9846755-7-9

www.paranormalcrossroads.com

Table of Contents

TATTOOTIE

Jo Hammers

Paranormal Crossroads & Publishing

CHAPTER ONE

A Rash From Tattoo Ink

Showering and scrubbing her skin roughly, Tattootie tried to remove some of the tattoo parlor inks from her skin. She was having a severe reaction to one of the products of her occupation. She was a tattoo model and just within the last week she had developed an allergy to inks. Overnight, the career she had created to earn cash for rent and the expenses of college ended. It was December. In January, she would enter her last semester of college. Now, she was suddenly without finances. As she shampooed her hair, she got lost in thought.

It was imperative now that she be creative and come up with a new way to earn cash. She had done it before. Three or so years prior she had heard a girl complain that the tattoo she wanted didn't look the same on her as it did on the paper in the tattoo artist's display book. She was going in for laser surgery to have it removed and was very disappointed concerning the experience. That is where she came up with the idea of being a tattoo model. She let the tattoo artist draw a quick rendition of the client's choice on her skin and body where ever the client wanted it. The tattoo artist used regular office ball point pens to draw on her and the client got to see what it would look like before they committed to it. The charge was a hundred dollars for her services and she split that with the artist. Larger tattoos that covered her face or a quarter of her body, she got three to four hundred dollars for the process. For three and one half years she had been a walking billboard of fake tattoos. They usually washed off by the end of the school week just in time to be inked again the next weekend. The pay was good and she made enough on Friday and Saturday nights to keep a roof over her head, food, and her college expenses paid. She was frugal and made every penny work for her and her future.

While scrubbing her skin to try to make herself a little more presentable, she decided a small personal loan would be enough to get her thru her last semester while she dreamed up another lucrative self created job. She only needed about nine thousand dollars. When she figured out another way to earn cash, she would concentrate on paying the bank loan back. She didn't want student grants or loans to pay back after college. She was going to be someone after college; not someone head over heels in debt. She already knew that flipping burgers in a fast food joint wouldn't provide her with the finances she needed. She had tried that when she was sixteen. College was expensive. She just hoped the loan officer at the bank was agreeable to helping her till she came up with a new idea.

Tattootie became her own best company and had lived in her own private world shutting the normal people, as she called them, out. William, her imaginary lover and friend, was the only individual allowed to be part of her inner social circle. The normal world rejected her so she avoided them. It wasn't unusual for her to talk to herself. Other than the tattoo parlor, she had very little social life. People saw her as a freak and not someone to be friends with. So, she told herself how nice she looked, that she was loved, and that she was someone every morning as she looked into the mirror at her reflection. William her imaginary friend always agreed with her as he stood wrapped in a pink towel having just exited the shower.

When you have been alone too long, sometimes you invent an imaginary friend. Lonely adults do it just as children do, they just don't talk about it. Tootie had an imaginary lover. A couple years before when she was a freshman in college, a stranger stopped in at the tattoo parlor inquiring as to the status of a vacant building next door. He stated that he was from the Park Street Bank and was repossessing their neighboring structure. Tattootie was instantly attracted to the older man in his forties. To the world he was a simple clean cut fairly tall Jewish businessman. To Tattootie he was the epitome of what a husband or a father should look like. He had a four o'clock shadow. It was late day and she was attracted to his end of along working day look. He had beautiful raven black hair and there was no doubting he would need to shave again before dinner. She could see him coming home to her every evening. She photographed him in her memory and accompanied him outside to discuss the future of the vacant building. She was a business major at the university. She saw it as an opportunity to learn a little about the world of banking and real estate.

Tattootie's body and face were covered with fake tattoos that afternoon. The banker was polite answering her questions, but showed no interest in her as a woman. With a shocked expression, he looked her over once, and then ignored her. She felt he saw her, like the other normals of society, as a person not worthy of befriending or taking seriously. It was just one more rejection. She had become accustomed to it. Ignoring his indifference to her, she took in every detail of his appearance down to the black lace up dress shoes he wore. He was delicious looking and she wanted him. She asked him casually whether he had a family. He smiled and told her that he had a wife and four children. Smiling, he pulled his wallet from his pocket and showed her a photo of his two boys and twin girls. He further shared the facts that his two older boys were soccer players and his twin girls were in to fashion dolls. It did not matter that he had showed no interest in her, she wanted him. She studied every detail about him as he taped his repo paperwork on the door of the vacant building. That night after the tattoo parlor closed, she took her new friend, an imaginary one, home with her to stay. The banker's image became her friend and lover.

Each and every morning, William leaned against her bathroom wall wrapped in a bath towel like a husband might if he were waiting for his turn at the single sink. This morning he was listening to her ramble in distraught as she tried to remove ink from her skin. He was a gentle man who always smiled and said "I understand. It is okay, Tootie."

"William, the ink from last night's tattoos isn't coming off!"

"It is okay, dear. Tattoos are your business." He replied.

"I guess I will have to face the loan officer as I am," she muttered eyeing the devil tattoo on the side of her face with its tail wrapped around her eye and eyebrow. She also had a red pimply rash on her arms and neck.

"You cannot let yourself be inked any more. You know what the skin doctor told you." William stated fiddling with his loosely wrapped pink towel. He was a handsome, dark skinned, Jewish man. William was everything to her. He was her secret.

Tattootie inspected her skin. She was one red dotted mess. The dermatologist she went to see earlier in the week stated that the inks were poisoning her. Her skin was absorbing their lethal chemicals into her system. The rash was a first warning. The doctor informed her that she would develop cancer and die if she continued. The prediction was frightening as well as a reality check. She had to find a new vocation. Strapped for cash, she knew that she had to finish out her week to have enough money to pay her December rent and put food on her table. Last night was her final night as Tattootie the Tattoo model.

"Look at yourself in the mirror, Tootie. You have a new walking display of tattoos as well as a serious rash. Your rash is worse. You should have quit the middle of the week when the dermatologist told you to do so." William stated shuffling his leaning position on the wall."You are going to dress skimpy to let the rash heal. It is freezing outside and I fear you will get frost bite."

"I know it is winter and also that the rash is worse."She replied."I will wear a skimpy top and short skirt."

Jo Hammers

After retrieving the skimpiest clothing she could find from her closet and putting it on, she returned to eye her reflection in the bathroom mirror. Her legs were covered with fake tattoos as well as her arms and face. In two or three days the fake tattoos would start to fade. However, her body looked a mess with the hodgepodge of unrelated tattoos. She had done pretty well in earnings for the previous day. She had made close to three hundred dollars. However, that wouldn't last long with it being December and close to Christmas.

The day after she had seen the dermatologist, she had filled out a bank application for a loan where she had her checking account. She only had one semester of college left and about five months of rent and necessities to cover. After that, she would have her degree in business management and she planned to open herself a successful business of some sort. She hadn't decided what yet. It definitely wouldn't be a tattoo business. She wanted to look normal, blend into society, and have a life where she was respected.

Picking up an old framed photo from her night stand, she thought about her parents whom she could barely remember. A case worker gave the snapshot to her when she turned fifteen. Her parents had died when she was three and had made absolutely no provisions for her future. She secretly didn't understand why they chose to have her and then be so selfish as to commit a double suicide leaving her behind. She had no siblings or grandparents on either side. She was a die, sink, or swim child. So far, she had managed to swim after running away from the last low class trashy foster home when she one day short of her sixteenth birthday.

Her teen and college years were spent in a tattoo parlor working as Tattootie the walking billboard. The general public saw her as a disgusting freak. Boys and men assumed she was easy and not serious date material. She had never had a boyfriend because she wouldn't date those in the gutter which seemed to be all that she attracted. She hated the male race and she had many reasons for it. She dreamed of a normal life with a house in the suburbs and a bathroom filled with pink bath towels. She was one semester of college and five months of rent away from having her dream.

Children were the one thing she didn't want. She never wanted to die suddenly and leave a child to go thru what she had been thru in the foster care system. Her plan was to be educated, travel, have a nice home, date possibly, but never marry. She had seen her share of bad marriages when she was bounced around amongst foster parents. She was going to live her life successfully and to the highest standard of normalcy she could manage. She planned to be a smiling, wealthy old maid in the suburbs planting flowers and eating vegetables from her little back yard garden. She might have a cat. She hadn't decided yet. Right now, she couldn't afford the cat food for one.

She finished dressing. The devil's tattoo around her eye was a scary one. The ink didn't fade with showering. She tried to wash it off with an application of cold crème. That was not successful. She would have to face the bank loan officer with the fake devil tattoo looking like it was going to jump off her face any moment and take the unsuspecting onlooker to Hell. She hated it. However, it had put a couple hundred dollars in her pocket last night. She was used to having images on her skin that she didn't particularly care for. It was part of the business. As she stared at the hideous devil, she put on her lipstick and then her jewelry. She was a normal woman. She just had fake tattoos all over her. She hoped that the loan officer didn't stare too much.

She gave up on staring at her reflection in the bathroom mirror. She made her way to her front door where she grabbed her coat, worn out stocking hat, and mittens. "Goodbye, William. Make sure you are home on time for dinner." She yelled.

She was surprised when she stepped out into the December morning. It was unseasonably warm. She would have to remember to tell William he was wrong about the morning weather. Her bare legs in short boots and socks would be fine. She needed to let her body rash air as the dermatologist had suggested. She had given up a long time ago on what people thought about her. Survival was her game and had been for around five years. In her morning choice of clothing, she looked a little bit like a punk rocker crossed with a goose bumpy teen wearing too little in too cold of weather.

"Think June and spring, Tootie. This nightmare will be all over and you can move to the life that you really want. This is just one more hurdle that you have to cross." She stated and then started her four block walk to the Park Street Bank.

Tootie tried to do all of her business close to where she lived. It was a lesson that she had learned quickly. Old cars could be drains on the pocket book. She rode public transportation to college and when it was necessary to visit other parts of the city. Otherwise, Park Street and its variety of businesses were her home and she lived in a tiny studio above an insurance office. The tattoo parlor where she worked was part of the night life scene in the same general area on a back street of bars and clubs.

CHAPTER TWO

Ward's Final Morning

Ward Goldman sat in his office at the Park Street bank kicked back in his chair with his feet up on his desk. This was his last day as bank president. He was taking early retirement and planned to write the book he had dreamed about his whole life. Although he was successful in his career in banking, it had never been what he wanted to do with his life. Now it was time to turn the reins of bank president over to someone else. He hadn't made up his mind who would inherit his office. It was a family business so there were only two choices, his nephew Stewart who worked in the loan department and his cousin William who ran a branch bank out in the suburbs.

As he sat there thinking, he was tried to make his mind up who would replace him. It had to be a relative as stated in his father's will and trust. He didn't particularly like his nephew Stewart. However, he was dedicated to the bank and was young enough that he could head the bank for twenty or more years. His cousin William, at the branch bank, had a wife and four children. He was a stalwart in the community. He volunteered and participated in practically every charitable event the community hosted. That was good for business. Stewart never volunteered for anything. He was in to whatever put a dollar in his and the bank's pocket. He disliked both of his relatives for different reasons. Having to choose, which one of the two would take over as bank president, wasn't easy. However, it was a choice he had to make it by the end of the business day.

Over the last five years, he had secretly hoped that his nephew Stewart would quit or get fired. That would have kept the monkey off his back. He would not have had to consider him for the position. In Ward's mind, Stewart was a self centered, little piss ant. He cringed at the idea of turning the family owned bank to him.

Equally annoying was his second choice for bank president. His cousin William was a great guy and banker but he had a blind side. His sneaky wife was a gold digger. Ward hated to see her get her clutches on the strings of the family fortune.

He was sure that his cousin didn't see his wife for what she really was. That made him equally as bad of a candidate as his nephew. There was no third choice.

His father's trust said that the bank presidency had to pass down to a male member who was employed in the bank. He only had two relatives working in the bank. One of the two was going to end up disliking him. His father's will and trust also stipulated that the one taking over could not have a juvenile or adult criminal record. It also stated that any documented theft was an automatic reason for the relative to be fired as well as not considered for the presidency of the bank and the theft charges didn't have to be proven in a court of law. His father's will and trust was simple. The person taking over the presidency had to work in the bank, be a relative, and couldn't have any record or be a thief. According to the trust set up by his father, the only way Stewart or William could be fired was for theft. If they were caught and documented, then they would lose their position at the bank as well as any inheritance from the family trust. His father had included a motel towel stolen was just cause for a dismissal.

Just before passing away, his father had installed security cameras in William's and Stewart's offices to spy on them. The cameras had a direct feed to a secured viewing system in Ward's office. He rarely peeped in on them, but he decided today was probably a good time to do it. He could leave in good conscience saying that he had monitored them before making his decision.

Unlocking a pair of folding cabinet doors, he removed the remote to turn on the direct link security view of William's office. He wasn't in there. He put the remote down temporarily, due to the fact he had a phone call.

"Ward Goldman speaking," he answered.

"Today is the day, you lucky dog. Are you looking forward to that book you have talked about writing when you retired? Your chance to become what you have always wanted to be is knocking at your door."

"Yes, William, I am excited about getting to do what I want instead of my father's choice for me. How are Betty and the kids?"

"They are fine. The boys are playing their violins in the Christmas program at church and the twin are little girls into fashion dolls. Betty hides in her art books. One of the boys is coming over to the main bank this morning to give you a retirement gift. He made it for you in his art class. Pretend you know what it is. It is made of clay and is suppose to be a huge gold dollar. I'm afraid it looks more like a gold painted hamburger patty. I think we are wasting our money giving him art lessons. Don't laugh when you see it.

"Does Betty still paint street scenes of men in cafes?' he asked thinking about the girl he once dated who dreamed of going to France and getting lost in the art scene. William had stolen her away from him and eloped with her. William was younger than Betty.

"You still don't hold that against me, my falling in love with your girl?"He asked. "Betty and I are really happy."

"You saved me an alimony check. I owe you one! I like food and she was a tofu eater. We would have divorced the first two weeks over the refrigerator, had we made it to the altar." Ward laughed.

"She still eats the strange stuff. You were asking if she still paints; she has a studio in our basement and an obsession with painting French street scenes. I don't understand that one, but I don't say anything. She wants to go to France on our vacation next year. I told her this morning absolutely not. We are going to Hawaii where I can get some much needed sunshine. You know how it is when you have been cooped up in a cubicle office all year. You don't want to spend your vacation in a bunch of stuffy art galleries."

"I hear you. I am planning a little trip to the Islands myself. I have office cabin fever too."

"My kids have no interest in art. They take their lack of culture after me. They would be miserable being dragged from art museum to art museum. Betty doesn't appreciate her children's non art talents. She keeps stuffing art lessons down their throats. My boys would rather have fishing rods and surf board lessons. The girls would like roller skates. However, all of us suck it up and put up with her insistence on art lessons and gallery visits. However, vacation in France is not flying with us."

"I can remember a time she had me wearing tie dye T-shirts. I feel for you. Looking back now, I think I must have been nuts for wearing the things." Ward replied.

"Have you made your decision as to which of us is to take over?" he asked pausing. "I want you to know that if you choose your nephew, it is okay with me. I have been fortunate to have had a good position with the bank all of these years and money to raise my family well. You have been good to me and I appreciate it. After your announcement, whichever way it goes, maybe all of my clan could join you in the Islands for a few days."

"Maybe my next trip to the islands, you and all your brood can join me. This first trip, I am finding me a pretty Hawaiian lady and blow some of my retirement savings. I have devoted my life to this bank. I am ready for a vacation and a little self indulgence. I plan on having a pretty Island girl or two on my arm. Your boys might not look up to me as much if they flew over and saw me with bare ladies me drunk as a skunk."

"It must be in our genes. I love Betty with all of my heart, but I keep having these night dreams about a dark haired girl who is constantly bathing. I stand in her bathroom with a towel around me and call her dear. My psychiatrist says I am having a mid-life crisis and the dreams will stop when Betty agrees to make love to me in the bath. I don't know why I go to him. I really think he is a quack but the dreams are so real. I can't tell Betty. She would see it as infidelity. What do you think is wrong with me?"

"You probably have a soul mate out there somewhere and it isn't Betty." laughed Ward. "Maybe I should take you to Hawaii with me. You could buy Betty a ticket for France. I think that we could probably round up a couple pretty ladies for the hot tub. You could parade your lily white body around in a bath towel while you soak up a little sun and some attention."

"I shouldn't have mentioned it. Betty would kill me if she knew this. I am happy in my marriage, Ward. However, I am even happier at night when I dream. I think I have a screw loose. I am in love with two women and one of them is just a dream.'"

"How long have you been dreaming about this woman?" Ward asked.

"I have been stalking her in my dreams for four or five years." He replied.

"Damn, William! You do have a screw loose. Do I know the woman?"

"I met her and spoke with her for ten minutes four or five years ago. I was repossessing the old Hancock building down in red light district. She was a dark haired vampire type, wore skimpy clothing, and had smudged ink all over her body. I went in where she worked and asked to borrow some tape to secure the repo notice on the Hancock building window. She walked outside and helped me tape up the notice. We talked for two or three minutes. I handed her the roll of tape and left. Now, I lean on her bathroom wall in my sleep in the nude wrapped only in a pink bath towel and watch her bathe and dress.

"A vampire girl, that is interesting. Is the pink towel yours or hers? "asked Ward laughing.

"That is just it, Ward. I don't know. I may be a fruit loop and don't know it. The psychiatrist thinks I should get one to see how it makes me feel in the morning. Can you imagine how that would go over with Betty?"

"Well, old pal. I think you need a vacation in the Islands as much as I do. Why don't you go down to where the vampire girl worked and take another look at her? Maybe it would cure your fantasy. In the past five years she could have birthed four kids and took a Harley riding husband with a pea shooter in his boot."

"I am totally committed to my marriage, Ward. I am not going to rock my boat for an uneducated, weird, shop girl. I would never find another Betty. She rocks my world."

"I need my world rocked. Do you want to share the night dream Vampire girl? Tell me where she worked and I just might become her pink toweled man and get you off the hook. I personally would love a woman who would take my bathroom and make it pink interesting. That damn decorator put gray towels in my bathroom. I hate them."

"Sorry, I think I will keep my night girl because I like her pink towel." William stated laughing." Well, I just called to tell you that I wish you the best."

"Thanks William. I will drop out at your branch and have a final lunch with you when I return from Hawaii. Who I choose for the Bank Presidency, won't take over till after Christmas."

"Just a thought, Ward, why does it have to be a family member run the bank. Had you ever thought about appointing a Vice President and giving them all of the president's duties and powers? You could remain president in name only, but still control the bank's future. Stewart and I neither one are experienced to do what you do. However, I do know someone that would make a great Vice President."

"Has Betty put you up to this little ploy to save the Presidency for you someday or one of your sons?"

"Well, asshole, I was referring to your Secretary Madge Burns. She had been your right hand man for fifteen years. There is no one more qualified!" He replied. "I am sorry that you feel that Betty interferes in my banking career. I now know that you have chosen Stewart. That is alright with me. However, you could make a better decision than both of us put together."

"I am sorry, William. I was hoping that you would see that you aren't qualified. I will have my secretary keep an eye out for Betty."

"I am sorry that Betty has stood between us all of these years. If I could go back, I would still marry her all over again, Ward. I really do love her. We have a really good life together. Losing you as my constant pal has been a great loss. Is there any chance we could have a better relationship now that we are getting older? I could visit you alone or we could golf. Damn, I have got to go. My other line is flashing. Have a good one, Ward!"

CHAPTER THREE

Ward Spies on Betty

Ward returned to the security monitoring system and pushed a button bringing up a view of the waiting area. There he watched and grinned as he watched William's little boy walk up and look at a lady with tattoos on her face. He leaned back in his office chair to watch for a few moments take a look at the boy's mother, Betty. Once upon a time, fifteen years earlier, he had been in love with her. She used him to keep a roof over her head and pick up the expenses of her last year in college. Then she dumped him for his cousin, William Goldman, whom she thought was going to take over the bank as Vice President.

When they were dating, he was studying to get his masters degree and was in no hurry to finish his education because he knew his father expected him to take a position at the bank. He always told her that he didn't want the presidency of the bank and that he intended to pursue a career in journalism. She saw him as becoming a starving writer living in a shack in the Islands somewhere. That wasn't her goal. She wanted to be married to someone who could afford to take her to places like France and Italy to study the great masters of art. William was a stupid young ass who fell for her 'I am madly in love with you routine'. A gold digger was what she was and still was in his opinion.

However, he couldn't help sneaking a peak at her. He still found her attractive, but the love was long gone. She had four children by his cousin and had been the family nightmare for years. When William's back was turned, she flirted with the other men in the family who were above her husband in social position. His father had warned him to stay clear of her and confided that she had tried to convince him as old as he was that she was secretly in love with him. His father had been seventy-two at the time and Betty twenty seven. She wanted to move up the social ladder even if it meant dumping naïve William who had a blind side. He lived and breathed Betty and their four children.

Viewing the security screen which was focused in on the reception area, Ward spotted Betty and admired what a beauty she was after having four children. Life hadn't taken a toll on her. She was just as attractive as the day she crushed his heart dumping him for his cousin. Seeing her always brought back painful memories. He avoided her as much as possible.

CHAPTER FOUR

Devil on Her Face

Tattootie was on time at the bank and patiently waiting. It seemed that the loan officer wasn't as prompt as she had disciplined herself to be. She knew that if she survived in the world on her own she had to play a respectful and smart game. Her looks hadn't got her where she was. Her wit and sheer determination had. Staying focused and being respectful had opened a few doors for her in spite of her obvious tattooed body.

As she sat there waiting, a seven or eight year old boy walked up to her asking, "Why do you have Jesus on the cross drawn on your arm and Satan on the side of you face with his tail wrapping around your eye?"

She grinned at him thinking how much he looked like a young version of her William. The boy had made a great observation and he was curious. She had been an inquisitive child always asking why. Her question had gotten her spanked, stood in corners, and made to do chores. Foster parents didn't like to be questioned about anything. You were a monthly welfare check to them and nothing more. You learned not to ask questions and to keep your mouth shut about what you were curious about.

Tootie started to answer his question when his mother jumped up from her waiting room chair, scurried to his side, and dragged him away. Tootie didn't look towards the woman, but she listened. The prim and proper suburb woman scolded him for talking to a stranger. Parents were jerks sometimes. The child had a great opportunity to learn about body art. Just because a child looks, it doesn't mean that an eight year old is going to run out and get a tattoo. She did, however, respect the mother's reference to stranger danger. She had lived in foster care. She knew what dangers there were out there in the gutter world.

Being shunned was a familiar price that she had paid for her occupation .She had become accustomed to being the victim of people showing their prejudices and fears. It was a price that she had paid for her education. One day, she would choose her friends wisely for their tolerance of others. The boy's mother would not be one of them.

Tattootie had learned one great lesson in Life. Listen to people. Sooner or later, what individuals were came out of their mouth. Humans painted pictures of themselves with their tongues. She never became friendly with anyone till she had known them for at least three months. People's looks and manners could be really deceiving. She learned that words are the paint by which men paint whom they really are. She knew that mother of the curious boy was using snobbery to make herself someone and she looked down on anyone that was not from her social position. She wanted to instill those same snobbish ideas in to as well as frighten her child. She was sure that the woman was very unhappy behind the mask she wore. Chances are, she married for wealth and not love. Tootie could tell. The woman showed no love to her child in her discipline. In Tootie's mind, the woman saw her child as a burden and not as a blessing.

CHAPTER FIVE

Betty Ponders

Betty Goldman sat ignoring her little boy who was sniffling next to her. She had been harsh with him and she knew it. There was no way in Hell that she was going to let him associate with the tattooed trashy woman in skin revealing clothing with a devil tattooed around her eye. However, being an artist she actually thought that some of the tattoos were quite artistic. Her love for and the participation in the art world had long been drained from her. When she married her husband, she envisioned a life of travel to France and Italy and walking in the steps of the old masters. What she got was a branch bank manager husband and four kids that she really didn't want

Recently, her husband William had been talking in his sleep to someone that he was calling dear. When she was younger, she had no trouble holding her own with any woman. However, she was sure that her husband William had met someone younger than her and that he was having an affair. In his sleep He spoke of her tattoos and the washing of her body. The tattoo woman was forcing her to face her fears.

She hadn't confronted William for fear of him asking her for a divorce which would leave her penniless. She had no money of her own and she had no intentions of moving out of their suburbia home and into a cheap apartment on the other side of town with four kids in tow. Getting a job was out of the question. She was not working for minimum wage somewhere to support four kids. She was going to dump him before he dumped her.

Hopefully, she would be heading to France with William's cousin, Ward, if she played her cards right. Ward was a multi millionaire and owner of the Park Street Bank. She had dated and lived with him in her younger days. They had shared an apartment her last year in college. Ward had never married. She was sure that he might still be attracted to her. She was counting on that. She planned to waltz into his office and declare her long lost love for him and offer to dump William and the children and run off to France with him.

She had dumped Ward in college for William. She really thought that Ward was going to turn out to be a loser and be disinherited by his father when they were young and in college. As it turned out, the rebel Ward did an about face and became a conservative successful banker abandoning his dreams of becoming a writer. William never moved up in the family bank. Ward's father left the bank entirely to Ward and his stocks and other wealth to Ward's three sisters. When she made her play for William, dumping Ward, she didn't expect things to turn out the way they had. For his years of service, William hadn't been left anything in the senior Goldman's will.

She had hoped William would at least move up to the presidency of the bank. However, she was friendly with Ward's secretary, Madge Burns, who had left it slip that Ward's nephew Stewart had the thumbs up for the position. She was not going down in flames with William dumping her after all she had put up with. She had made love to a man for fifteen years that she despised and had children that she didn't want. Her dreams of being rich, socially upward mobile, and someone in the community was going was bellying up. She suddenly had no claims to the bank's future if William walked and dumped her. She had to look out for number one. She wasn't going to live and die in a cheap ass apartment for the elderly on the wrong side of town. Ward was now her focus. She was sure that he still had feelings for her or he would have married. Plus, his secretary had told her that he had developed diabetes. Maybe he had one foot in the grave and she could walk away with his fortune as well as the bank one day.

She patiently waited ignoring her child's sniffling. If she were Ward's wife, she could just walk past the nincompoop, half witted, hall guarding receptionist and tell her to go to hell. As William's wife, she had no clout. She was going to rectify that. She was going to convince Ward that she was still in love with him and that they should die old together in France leaving Park City behind. Ward was retiring today and she had to get to him before he took off to Hawaii and hooked up with some blonde beach bimbo. She hadn't planned on having to drag a sniffling kid along. He had complained of a headache when he got up. William had insisted that he be kept home. She hated her children who were strangling ropes around her neck. They were tolerable when she thought they were going to inherit part of the Goldman fortune. That didn't happen.

So, here she sat having to wait for a mealy mouthed receptionist to tell her it was okay for her to go back to Ward's office because she didn't have an appointment.

CHAPTER SIX

Is There a Problem

Ward Goldman sat in his office chair flipping a remote watching the different areas of the bank on security feed to a screen in his office. He didn't have anything overly important on his agenda. He was just trying to put in time till five. He had a plane ticket for an evening flight to Hawaii and his suitcase was in the trunk of his car.

"Well Betty," he said watching her on the security screen."Hopefully, this is the last time I will ever lay eyes on you. I am going to vacation for a couple of weeks and then I am going to come back and close all of my accounts, sell my house, and move to the Islands. I just don't see what William sees in you. You are a textbook gold digger. I was blind when I was young and in college. One of these days when Stewart is made president and your William doesn't move up, you will make a wrong move and William will see you for the leach you are. I would give him the presidency if it wasn't for you."

He continued to scan the different bank area just for the heck of it. After a little flipping of the remote he returned to the reception area. There he watched Betty's son walk over and speak with a tattoo covered young woman. Then he watched perfectly dressed Betty hurry over, forcefully grab her son by the arm, and drag him away from the woman. He pushed his buzzer for the receptionist.

"Step into my office a moment, please."Ward stated when the receptionist answered.

A few seconds later the receptionist entered his open office door. "Yes, Mr. Goldman?"She inquired.

"There is a little boy out in the lobby who just spoke with a tattooed woman. Is there a problem?"

"He is William's little boy. His mother is out there waiting to see you. I think they have brought you a retirement gift. They have a package with them."

"Why did William's wife grab the little boy and drag him away from the tattooed woman?" he asked.

"I heard her tell the boy to stay away from the lady with the tattoos because they were upper class, not gutter trash." She replied

"Did the tattooed woman say anything to invoke that response from William's wife?"

"No, the little boy walked over and asked the tattooed woman why she had Jesus on the Cross tattooed on one arm and the Devil on the side of her face. It was just idle child curiosity. The woman smiled at him and was about to tell him when his mother pulled him away."

"I see! Is the woman a client of the bank?" he asked.

"Yes, she has had a checking account with us for about five or so years. She owns her own business and is one semester away from graduating college. She is here applying for a small loan. I have spoken with her a few times over the years. She is a very nice person under all the tattoos."

"Thank You. Tell William's wife that I have left the office by the back door and send her away. I don't want to see her. Close my door when you leave."

"Yes, Mr. Goldman," she replied and left closing the door.

He returned to the security screens. He flipped the remote causing it to pull up his nephew Stewart's office. He wanted to take one last look at him and how he handled customers. He had pretty well decided to turn the presidency of the bank over to him. William was qualified, community minded, and would make a great bank president. He was not the problem. Ward just didn't want Betty to stick her hand in the till any further than it already was.

On the security screen he eyed Stewart doing some paper shuffling. He left the screen on there as he pulled some breath mints from his pocket. Since he had been diagnosed with diabetes it seemed that he had a constant problem with his breath. When he reached Hawaii, he planned to exercise, start a diet, and try to get his health under control. No woman would want to date him in his current condition and with his health issues. If he wanted to grow old with someone, he knew that he was going to have to make some drastic changes. He had hired a trainer in Hawaii and he planned on a two week crash diet as well as an exercise program. He was out of shape, overweight, and was borderline having to go from pills to insulin. The two weeks in Hawaii were important. He couldn't let anyone or anything stand in the way of that. His doctor had but all chewed him a new asshole when he went in for his checkup. His blood sugar was up over two hundred heading for three and his blood pressure was also an issue.

He popped a breath mint in his mouth and watched Stewart for the heck of it. He knew that he had a client on the schedule that was to arrive any moment.

CHAPTER SEVEN

Tattootie Meets Stewart

"Tootie Beecham," the receptionist called loudly.

Tattootie glanced up at the call of her name.

"Mr. Goldman is ready for your now. Follow me." she said pointing to the long haul behind her desk.

Tattootie rose and circled the desk to follow her. Halfway down the short hallway, the receptionist pointed to an open door and waited for her to enter and then she stepped in behind her .The dark paneled office with its golfing scenes was definitely a man's cave. She took a quick glance about while the receptionist handed the loan officer a folder.

"Mr. Goldman, this is Tootie Beecham your ten o'clock client."

"Thank You, Sarah. Don't close the door." He stated eyeing Tattootie over the top of his gold, wire rimmed glasses. He couldn't have been over twenty five. However, he looked like an old man the way he peered over the top of his rims. Then he did the strangest thing. He looked over at one blank wall and winked like he had something in his eye.

Tattootie bit her lip to keep from snickering. She wondered if this young, good looking, Jewish loan officer might have a screw loose. She had seen her share of screwballs on the streets. Down on fifth there was a street man who hung out in front of a restaurant winking at ladies as they entered on their lunch breaks. His twitching eye netted him a lot of soft drinks and sandwiches. She wondered what the loan officer's game was winking at a blank wall.

The loan officer abandoned his wall winking and turned her way. He eyed her tattoos and skimpy clothing with a smirk on his face. Tootie could tell that he was disgusted with her appearance. He, like the boy's mother, would have prejudiced social blinders on seeing only his world of finance, fine restaurants, and Saturday golf. She instantly had a gut feeling and knew he was a snob. He would date only girls with money and status. A poor girl, or one like herself, would never be considered by him. She was sure about her quick assessment of him.

"There is no need for you to sit down, Miss Beecham, or to waste my time. You have no collateral and your occupation, in my thinking, is a phony one. I am tired of transients and street people like you waltzing in here tying to con me and the bank out of money to buy drugs or who knows what." He stated not even asking her to sit down.

"I beg your pardon. I am not a transient or a street woman. My application is legitimate. I have worked as a tattoo model for five years and I have tax returns to prove it."

"In my opinion, Miss Beecham, you are white street trash looking for money for a quick fix. Now get out of my office and take your con game elsewhere." He replied rising.

"You are reading me all wrong, Mr. Goldman. I am a business woman and my request is a legitimate one. I turn my earnings in to the IRS the same as you and pay my taxes." She shot back.

"Take your phony application and your line of bull shit elsewhere. This bank makes loans to decent, hard working, legitimately employed individuals, not tattoo freaks and harlots in short skirts."

"You, Mr. Goldman, are a little man in a three piece suit who has probably never worked a regular job in your life or had compassion on anyone you saw as less than you. You are the white trash, not me. White trash has no regard for others."

"If you walk like a duck, you are a duck, Miss Beecham. You are dressed, and look like a tattooed street walker. Take your duck label and wear it."He shot back once more winking at the blank bank wall to the side of his desk.

"It takes a duck to know a duck, I suppose. That cup in your hand belongs to the clubhouse restaurant where you golf. It has its logo on it. You stole it or you wouldn't have it in your possession. I worked there briefly a few years ago. They don't sell their cups. You have to steal one to have it in your possession. You tell me how you got it. Was it a quick slip into your golfing sweater's pocket? You are a thieving duck." she retorted with her face flushed.

"How dare you insinuate that I am a thief!" he half yelled.

"You walk like a duck, Mr. Goldman, you are a duck. You sit there drinking from a stolen duck's cup. You are a thieving duck."

"Get out of my office." He yelled and once more winked at the wall.

"Good Day, Mr. Goldman. Karma one day will come back to you and bite you in the butt. I hope I am around to see it." Tootie then spun on her heel, held her head high, and walked out paying no attention to a well dressed Jewish man standing at the door waiting to enter.

"You are tattooed trash!" yelled the loan officer after her.

Tattootie turned briefly stating, "I am a legitimate business woman who will now close my accounts with your bank. I believe in Karma. One day soon you will be in my shoes. It is the law of the universe, what you sow, you reap." Then she turned and left passing the nicely dressed man in the hall who was about to enter.

CHAPTER EIGHT

Ward's Confrontation with Stewart

Edward Goldman watched the tattoo covered young woman exit the hallway of the bank's offices and leave. She had been so intent on berating his nephew that she was oblivious to his standing at the door. Pausing a moment, he watched her exit the hall. He had to find out who she was. There was something about her that he found very appealing. He stepped in to his nephew's office.

"Don't mind the freak," stated Stewart pointing to a chair for his uncle and winking. He was sure that he had come to give him the news that he was taking over as president of the family bank and to tell him that the tattoo woman was a plant by the bank examiners. "What is on your mind?"

Edward Goldman didn't sit down. "I was doing a scan of the security cameras and was surprised to tune in on your little episode with the tattoo woman. Our bank, Stewart, makes its money collecting interest on loans to small business owners like her. All the little people's loans add up and pay your salary as well as mine and the other employees. Your treatment of her was uncalled for. I watched on the security monitor."

"She is a freak, bank examiner's plant." Stewart interjected "I threw her out because I knew you were watching me."

"There was a bank examiner's plant. She came thru first thing this morning. You just demeaned one of our long time checking customers. She has been with the bank almost five years according to Sarah."

"Don't get pissed off, Ward. She is white trash and not worth worrying about."

"All of our customers are worth worrying about. We are not the judge of their lives. We judge collateral and credit scores. I am sure that everyone in the reception area heard you calling her white trash. That is not acceptable even if you thought she was a plant."

"Okay, I have pissed you off. What else do you want to talk to me about?"

"The tattoo woman has pointed out an item of interest that must be considered in my choice for president of the bank. In father's trust, he stipulates that anyone caught stealing cannot move up to bank president. The trust also stipulates that the theft does not have to be bank related. Your so called tattoo freak was kind enough to point out your theft of a coffee cup from the golfer's club. A thief is a thief. In accordance with father's trust, I am firing you for theft. A man stealing a little thing will continue to pilfer till he moves up to larger things. The security guard will be here in ten minutes to escort you out. " Ward stated who wanted his nephew to get a taste of the real world.

Stewart was at a loss for words and stood with his mouth open for a moment in shock and then yelled, "You can't fire me! Who will run the bank?"

"William," Ward replied firmly.

"You will regret this, Uncle Edward!"

"I don't think so. To be honest, I don't like you! I have only kept you on out of respect to my dead sister, your mother."

"You aren't exactly my favorite relative either," Stewart shot back mad.

"Your file will list theft as your reason for dismissal. Your conversation with the tattoo lady is documented on security tape." Edward Goldman stated." Not only are you a thief but you crossed all the lines in the treatment of a customer."

Then Ward Goldman president and owner of the Park Street Bank turned and walked out leaving Stewart sputtering and yelling obscenities behind him.

CHAPTER NINE

Tootie Meets Ward

Furious, but controlling her anger, Tootie exited the long hallway and then left the bank. Once outside of the bank building, she leaned against the cold block building for a moment to compose her flustered nerves. She hadn't prepared herself for such a demeaning, rude, prejudiced encounter as she had just experienced. She wondered how the extremely rude man about her age kept his job. When she managed to start herself a business after her last college semester, customers would be treated respectfully no matter how they looked.

She spotted a familiar bus bench. She walked over and sat down to think. Bus benches were great places to sit and think. They had been her living room couch when she first ran away. She had sat on a lot of them when she needed to rest and think. Here she was again, needing her couch's solace and comfort. Someday when she purchased her house in the suburbs, she was going to purchase one of these benches and have it installed in her flower garden. She had programmed herself to think on them. She wasn't sure that she could live in suburbia without one.

"Think, Tootie! You have a brainstorm in you somewhere that can create a new way of making the finances you need. You knew better than to fill out that application to begin with. You know what people like Goldman are like. You have had five years of learning the hard way. They are only there for themselves and those they deem appropriate.

Then, she muttered to herself," Someday if it is in the cards, I want to burn your ass Mr. Goldman. I want to be the arm of Karma for once in my life instead of being the victim."

Fifteen minutes or so passed as she sat thinking on the public bus bench. It wasn't unusual for her to sit a couple of hours. When you needed to think, you needed to think. This was one of those times. However, sitting in her short skirt was a bit chilly. She pulled her coat around her and her stocking hat a little lower. As a survivor you learned that you didn't dress for fashion on the streets. You dressed for warmth and dryness. What she had on was a necessity to let her skin heal, but it definitely wasn't for bus bench sitting. She might have to cut her thinking a little short this morning.

A well dressed, heavy, middle aged gentleman walked up and sat down on the bus bench next to her. "It is a beautiful day, isn't it?"

"It would be better if I could figure out how to get thru my next semester of college without starving or being thrown out in the street for lack of rent money. I lost my job this week."

"Are you hitting me up for money?" he asked looking at the sky as though hoping for snow. In the banking business he always cut to the chase.

"No, I am just running at the mouth. I am not a panhandler. I actually just quit a job that I worked at for the last four, almost five, years."

"Twenty years for me. I am quitting today." he stated seemingly unconcerned about her appearance.

"My tattoos don't scare you off or repulse you?" She asked out of curiosity looking the round Jewish man in a business suit over. She liked the way he was heavy. Butterballs had to be normal because they were well fed. She could see herself with a butterball man in the suburbs hosting a back yard barbecue. He was actually quite handsome, just extremely over weight.

"Your tattoos are not real. I can tell." He replied. "I figure you work in some sort of art related occupation that requires them. Am I right?"

Tootie was taken back. "You are absolutely right. I have been working as a tattoo model to pay for my college expenses."

"I like people and try to guess what they are like. I would say you are a street smart survivor with goals."

"My days in the world of survival are about over. I graduate college in May and I am moving to the suburbs and start myself a whole new life."

"Good for you!" He replied. "Do you live with your parents?"

"My parents died when I was three. After a miserable childhood in foster care, I ran away the day before my sixteenth birthday. Since then, I have worked as a tattoo model and have managed to put myself thru high school and three plus years of

33

college. I am a survivor who has just hit a temporary snag. I will get past it."

"I wish I had insisted my nephew work for his education. He thinks life owes him and that I do to. He is full of himself and to be honest, I don't like him very much. He is my sister's kid and I feel I owe him. I have no children and have picked up the tab for whatever he has asked. He is spoiled and I am guilty of part of it.

"Sometimes, you have to cut family ties." She replied. "Maybe he needs a dose of reality check."

"Some definite changes have been made. I just fired him and he is not a happy camper at the moment. That is the reason I have come down here. I am giving him a chance to clear out his things." He stated looking again at the sky. "Don't you think that it is unseasonably warm for December?"

"Actually, I was thinking the same thing earlier. However, this short skirt is saying something else. I think I am going to have to give up my bus bench sitting and thinking."

"I kind of like this bench myself. I work in one of those upstairs offices behind us. Today is my last day. I will be officially unemployed at five this evening."

"Aren't we a pair?" she replied laughing. "The unemployment line calls us."

"My health is the reason for my position in the unemployment line. I have recently been diagnosed as diabetic and I am on the verge of a serious stroke or coma. My blood sugar is out of control"

"That is a bummer."

"My health issues are the hammer ending my career."

"I am so sorry, I wish there was something I could do for you." She replied. "We definitely are a pair. I have developed an allergy to the tattoo artists' inks they use on my skin. My dermatologist says that my system is absorbing the ink and it is poisoning me. This rash is the first sign that I will die from the inks if I continue. Last night was my last night as a tattoo model. I am sitting here trying to come up with a new idea to reinvent myself and create a new occupation that I can make decent money at. I like being an entrepreneur. "

"How long will these fake tattoos stay on your skin?" He asked eyeing the devil one on her face with his tail wrapped around one of her eyes.

"It will take about a week of showering and they will all start to fade and wash off. Two weeks from now, I will start to look normal again."

"Just the thought of tattoo needles makes me shiver. Right now I am on pills for my diabetes. The doctor says I need to get my weight and sugar under control or I am going to have to start giving myself insulin injections. I cringe at the thought." He replied.

"Do you know why your weight is out of control and your sugar is high?" she asked.

"I can't cook. I live alone and basically eat most of my meals in a restaurant. The food you get there isn't prepared according to diabetic guidelines. I will also admit that I am a big man and I like to eat, especially donuts."

"We both have our problems don't we." She replied. "What is, or was your occupation?"

"I have spent my life being a gopher for my father in our family business. "He replied. "I have always wanted to be is a writer."

"Family businesses can be a pain. I don't understand why fathers want their sons to follow in their footsteps. James, down at the tattoo parlor, is the son of the owner. His father expects him to take over the tattoo business. James wants to be a truck driver. He is miserable in the shop and would be even more so if he took over the business. He has the call of the road in his blood. I imagine you are like James."

"You nailed me!" he replied."However, at five o'clock this afternoon, I am a free man. My cousin, William, is taking over the family business."

"You need to sell surf boards or something of that nature on a beach somewhere. Business would be slow and you could write your book between customers. When you go to the beach, you don't seem to think so much about food. Something cold to drink is about all you want. That would be good for your weight and sugar problem. When you think of dieting to get health issues under control, just the thought of denying yourself makes you want to eat ten times a day."

"You are one smart little cookie." He replied grinning at her. "Edward Goldman is my name. My friends call me Ward."

"I am Tootie Beecham! In the world of tattoos, Tattootie is the name I go by. You can call me Tootie."

"Could I buy you a cup of coffee? There is a coffeehouse a couple shops down."

"Sure! Why not? Perhaps you can help me come up with a money making idea. I seem to be temporarily in a brain fog." She stated rising from the bench as he did.

He pointed the way and she joined him pulling her coat around her. She wished she had worn leggings. She was chilled.

"I will help you brain storm, if you will tell me about your life in the tattoo business. I like interesting people. I would like to write a book someday about all the unique people I have met.

"I read a lot. Which of your unique encounters would you write about?"She asked.

"I just might write about you and your crazy world. You are by far the most interesting person that I have met in awhile."

"You are the nicest person I have met in awhile. Usually, people ignore me or look at me in disgust like a woman did earlier in the reception area of the bank. She judged me by these fake tattoos and jerked her little boy away from me like I was the plague."

"I am an aging, brain dead, desk warmer who needs to reinvent his life, what is left of it. I have always dreamed of being an author."

"How old are you?" she asked.

"I am forty- two!"He replied stretching the truth a little. He was actually fifty.

"You don't have to lie to me. I have been on the streets and can read people. You bet your lip when you said forty-two. If I were guessing, I would read you as fifty and that you wish you were college age again so you could get your life right. Am I right?"

"You are dead on. Are you going to be my new mid life crisis guidance counselor?"

"I will be yours if you will be mine. In case you are wondering, I am almost twenty two. However, I feel like a hundred and two today. My problems are aging me."

"I feel like a hundred and fifty." He replied grinning."

"You grow up fast when you run away and hit the streets. Surviving will age you."

"Working at a job I have hated for twenty some years has put this gray in my hair. I have breathed, ate, and slept in my office. I am a compulsive workaholic and it has aged my body. I have health issues."

"I lived in foster care's low class rat traps I have slept in dumps on couches where no child should have ever been housed. . .I ran away and left the social service scene and their white trash behind when I was sixteen. In the last home that I was placed in, I had a foster father who just wouldn't leave me alone. It was either run away or be raped."

"How did you survive, being so young?"

I lived on top of a laundry building for about a year. I climbed up the fire escape ladder each evening after dark. It provided me free rent till I got caught. I managed to get away from the owner and ran. By that time, I was starting to make money in the tattoo business. I rented myself a cheap apartment downtown."

"What about your real parents?" he asked opening the coffee house door for her.

"I entered the foster care system when I was three. My parents killed themselves, a double suicide. I don't know why. Secretly, I think it was selfish of them to do it with no regard to what would happen to me."

"It sounds like you have done alright for yourself, in spite of them. You sound like a self made woman!"

"I have had to be. I have no one to fall back on."

"I tip my hat to you, Miss Tootie. I once knew a girl who was like you who was an art student. We met at the university. I was mad about her and she moved in me. She used me for a year of tuition and books and then dumped me for my cousin. A free ride was all I was to her. She was going thru college on grants and barely scraping by. My cousin was taking over the family business twenty years ago. She tossed me aside for someone whom she thought would have more money and social status than me. I just wanted to be a writer and hole up in a small apartment somewhere. You, however, are carrying your own weight. I respect that. I would like to find a woman my age who would love me for me. Every woman I have ever dated has loved my money."

"The money you no longer have," she replied laughing. "You quit your job, today, remember?"

"You are absolutely right. I am unemployed." He laughed eyeing the twinkle of mischief in her eye.

"Yesterday, I was a successful tattoo model. Tomorrow is an opportunity to become a new form of success. I just haven't figured out what yet. It will come to me. I am a thinker."

Ward pointed her to a little booth in the back and they seated themselves and ordered.

"Do you suppose you could do a little of that thinking for me? I could use a little reinventing myself."

"I will help you if you help me? She replied. "There are no free rides in this world, anyway I haven't found one."

So, the two spent a couple of hours in the little booth discussing business ideas and getting to know each other. However, Ward did not tell Tootie what his family business was. He led her to believe he was a pencil pushing desk salesman. He stayed clear of his last twenty years in the banking business. He wanted her to like him for himself, a simple unemployed man. When Tootie excused herself to use the facilities, he called his secretary and told her that he wouldn't be back in.

Having lived in totally different worlds, they enjoyed listening to each other's oddities and became friends. Tootie saw him as a butterball man she would be happy living in the suburbs with and having butter ball children she would have to hide the cookie jar from. She liked the way he looked. To her he was suburbia normal and that was what she wanted. Ward saw her as the woman he wanted on his arm on the beach for his retirement years. He also for the first time thought about having a child. He could see himself with three little girls all as interesting and beautiful as their mother. After a couple hours of conversation ignoring the passing of time, they parted carrying each other's phone numbers written on paper napkins. Both were sure that they had met that once in a lifetime special someone. The chemistry was there for both of them.

CHAPTER TEN

Betty Plots

Ward opened the back door to the bank and stepped inside wanting to avoid the reception area. To his dismay, Betty was standing just inside the door all smiles. He cringed on the inside. Her cornering him at the back door couldn't be a good thing. She was probably going to bend his ear with all the reasons that William should be made president of the bank. He bit his lip.

"Avoiding me?" she asked after telling her son to go get lost in the lobby and play with some toys that were there.

"I have been out for coffee with one of the bank's clients, if it is any of your business and it isn't," he replied smugly. After all these years, she still acted like she owned him. He had to be halfway civil because of William.

"I want to know who you are going to make President. William and I have a lot at stake on this promotion." She spit out.

Annoyed at her interference and wanting to piss her off he said, "Go home Betty, it won't be William."

"That does it then. I am not going to live with a loser who wants to spend all of his vacations lying on the beach in the hot sand in Hawaii." She stated frowning.

"What do you mean?" Ward asked not believing his ears. She had played the happy little loving wife of William the banker for years.

"I intend to divorce your cousin, take my half of our assets, and choose some handsome man to travel with me and live in France which was my plan before your Cousin seduced me. Being married to a branch bank manager doesn't cut it with me. Do you know that he doesn't even have a real office? He has a cubby hole behind the teller line that once was a supply closet. Without becoming president and moving over here to your office suite, he is nobody."

"You are going to divorce William because he isn't getting a promotion?" he asked in shock secretly knowing that he intended to give the presidency to him.

"He doesn't make enough money in that position to put braces on the twins teeth and give them ballet lessons. I have had it with the whole happy house wife scene. I made a mistake marrying him. He got me drunk and dragged me to a justice of the peace and married me. I didn't even remember the event I was so drunk. However, he was more than happy to show you the marriage certificate. I should have got an annulment and the two of us went on with our plans."

"I am sorry to hear that Betty. William called earlier and he has the impression that you have a marriage made in Heaven. I seem to remember the eloping event a little different than you. I believe it was William that was dragged to the altar drunk. However, he seems to be happy with you. Do you plan on taking the kids to France with you?"

"They were William's fantasy, not mine. He can have them and raise them. I could care less if I ever see him or them again. I do not plan on returning from France."

"Why are you telling me?"He asked wanting to get away from her, return to his office, and put in his last three or so hours.

"You are retiring. How would you like to go to France with me? We were good together once upon a time. I remember you liking certain erotic charms I offered in the bedroom?"

"You have got to be kidding! You dumped me for my cousin and told me to take a hike because I wasn't going anywhere in life. I believe that is how I recall it." He spit out pissed that she would even consider making such a suggestion.

"Think about it. It could be a new beginning for us. You are worth millions. We could live well in France, now that you are retiring. We don't need William," she stated running one of her fingers up his arm.

About that time her little boy cam running back whining that he was hungry.

"Take the child home, Betty." I definitely don't want one of William's children hearing this conversation. How could you say these things in front of the child?"

"We can be young again in France and carefree."She replied removing her finger from his coat sleeve. She then kissed the tip of it and placed it on a shocked Ward's lips."I will call you when the kids are in bed tonight. I am not taking no for an answer. We are just late in finding each other. We will pretend that William and the kids never existed."

Ward opened the back door for her. She grabbed the whining child by the hand and escorted him out batting her eyes in a flirty fashion at Ward.

CHAPTER ELEVEN

Ward Panics

After she left, Ward leaned for a few moments on the wall. He had a whole new can of worms to sort out. Stewart was a thief and William would be paying alimony out the yang-yang if he moved him up to the presidency of the bank. He was between a rock and a hard place and three hours to go till he was expected to make a decision.

In the shock of Betty's unexpected proposal, he momentarily forgot about Tattootie. He scurried to his office in a panic. He closed the door and plopped down into his office chair without taking his Jacket off. He had to make some a new decision quick. Tattootie and the number on a napkin in his jacket pocket was the last thing on his mind. He spun about in his swivel office chair and faced the security screens. He hoped that the bank camera security system had recorded the back door event. He couldn't figure out how to pull the tape up. He then spun back around to his desk and rang the security company asking them if they could pull the footage at the back door for the last thirty minutes and isolate a conversation he had with a woman with a little boy in tow. They said they would get back to him in fifteen minutes. In all the activity and movement of his chair, the napkin fell out of his jacket and on to the floor and slid under the side of his desk. He had no idea he lost it.

Next, he called William. It was time that his cousin wised up to his wife's deceptions. He was going to nip this thing once and for all in the bud. Betty didn't know that she had been standing under one of his father's prized dime sized security cameras. It would be up to William what to do with the information. Maybe William would see how he had been the victim of deceit and he would be open to exploring their being cousins and friends again. Betty had driven a wedge between them. He rang William at the branch bank.

"Park Street branch, William speaking," he answered.

"I am glad I caught you. I have caught something important on the security cameras and I need to have your take a look at it. Could you leave the branch in care of your tellers and scoot over here. I think you will want to see this. I can't put it off till I return from my trip. It is a security issue."

"It sounds serious by the sound of your voice. Should I tell my head teller to lock up later that I won't be back for the day?"

"I am afraid so, William. It is going to shock the hell out of you. Be prepared. Bring a tranquilizer and your checkbook and your stock portfolio with you. We are going to need to make some quick financial decisions. Don't tell Betty. You have got to keep this under wraps until tomorrow. This is top secret and has to do with my decision. I fired Stewart, in case you haven't heard."

"I will be right there." He stated and hung up the phone.

CHAPTER TWELVE

Ward's Proposal

Ward tapped a pencil on his desk thinking. He could see only one way to free him from the Presidency of the Park Street Bank. Stewart was gone and He couldn't appoint William because of the gold digger. It was a hard decision, but he was going to do it. He was sure that his secretary would go alone with it once she heard the deal. However, he dreaded telling Tootie why he had made his unusual decision. When you are responsible for a lot of people, sometimes you have to make no nonsense decisions. This was going to be one of them. He would explain it to Tootie as soon as he returned from the fat farm in Hawaii. Something in him told him that she was the one that he had been looking for all of his life, that special someone.

Ward pushed the buzzer for Madge his private secretary.

"Yes, Mr. Goldman," she replied.

I want you in here now. Comb your hair and bring us both a stiff cup of coffee. The Public Relations is on his way up to take some photos that I am going to release to the press. I know that you have been running around like a chicken all day doing my last day of crappy jobs picking up my laundry and dry cleaning. I know the wind outside is fierce and you probably need to go to the hair dresser, but there isn't time. Comb your hair, paint your lips, and get in here in a hurry."

"Yes Sir!" she replied in a confused quick reply.

In about five minutes, Madge Burns entered carrying two mugs of steaming coffee. She had her hair combed, lipstick on, and a confused look on her face. "Here is your coffee, Mr. Goldman. Do you want to fill me in on what is going on? I gather you are possible going to announce who is going to be president of the bank?"

"Sit down, Madge. This is going to be a shocker to you. Yes, I have decided and

I have our public relations man on his way up here. I have a tape I want to show you and then I am going to tell you what my decision is. You know that dad installed security cameras and a sophisticated taping system before he passed away. Well, watch this. Afterwards, you will know why I can't appoint William to the presidency. You already know that I have fired Stewart."

"Yes sir, I am aware that William is your only choice."

Well, watch this!"He stated playing the tape of him and Betty in the back door entrance.

"Holy Moses!" she replied half way thru the three minute taped episode. "Your father was right. She is a gold digger. He told me that she had propositioned him about seven or so years ago. I thought he was just an old man dreaming. No wonder he installed the cameras."

"Madge, you were my father's secretary before you became mine. I know that you are three years away from drawing social security and retiring. I have an offer to make you."

"Are you asking me to leave or firing me like you did Stewart? I know that Betty always makes a beeline for my desk when she is here. However, we are not friends. I have never particularly cared for her."

"No, I want you to accept the temporary position of bank president until William can free himself of her. He will take over as president the day you are eligible for your social security. At half a million a year, your social security pension amount would sky rocket. If you save the next three years salary, you could retire quite nicely. I need time to groom William as well as help him get a divorce from Betty. My plan is to demote William to the teller line. Her alimony based on teller's wages will be next to nothing, maybe six thousand a year. Are you willing to be a fill in bank president for three years?" William will work under you after his divorce is final as Vice president learning the ropes. You will teach him."

"Oh God, no wonder you told me to comb my hair." She replied laughing. "This is going to be one shocker to the employees as well as William and Stewart. How are you going to get by with this? The terms of the trust and your father's will are set in stone. It states that only a male relative that is a bank employee for at least five years or your wife or child can be appointed?"

I think a pre-nuptial marriage contract between you and I should set the ball in motion. I will marry you and then appoint you president. You can live out in my house in the suburbs for the next three years. I will take an apartment downtown.

It will be strictly a contract marriage although we might occasionally attend bank functions together to keep Betty at bay and everyone guessing. I want it to look like that you will be president till the day you die. Only you and I will know that we have the three year pre nuptial marriage contract and terms for your being president. You will type up the contract and we will sign and have it notarized across town at some notary that doesn't know us. You will get no alimony, or other benefits. What you will get is the notoriety of being a bank president and three years of a half million dollars in salary."

"Sir, you do realize that I am a lesbian and have a secret lover? My marriage to you could pose some problems should anyone find out about my sexual preference."

"No marriages are perfect. You can have your lover and I will have mine. We will never sleep together. We will just dote on each other when we are in the public eye. You can take your lover out to my estate and tell everyone she is your maid or something. "

"Three years on the love boat out in your mansion sounds like a winner to me. My Callie is going to think that we have hit the big time. She works at a fast food restaurant."

"I have a housekeeper, Madge. I want to keep her on. I can't divulge our fake marriage to her, so you will just have to put up with her stares and disapproval. She will think that you are playing around on me if she catches you in bed with Callie. Limit your love making to nights, weekends, and after five when she has gone home."

"Keep one faithful housekeeper in the dark. I have got it, boss."

"After all these years, I have met someone, Madge. I haven't known her very long, but I know she is the one for me. At the same time, I can't retire without a president. You are the only one qualified. The only way I can appoint you, is to marry you."

"Well, Mr. Goldman. You are not my sexual preference, but I think we are going to have a very happy three year contractual marriage. I will tolerate your lover if you tolerate mine."

"I just want everything to be up-front! After I return from the fat farm in Hawaii I hope to have my lady friend move in with me and marry her the day you and I divorce three years from now."

"I won't let you down, Ward. I will look for ways to make my salary back for the bank. This is an opportunity for me. I appreciate the chance to prove myself after all these years. I may double my own million and a half."

"I should have seen your talents for what they were years ago. I have had my head up my yang. William pointed out to me your qualifications" he replied taking out a pocket comb and combing his own jet black Jewish hair.

"May I ask how you are going to explain that I am ten years older than you?" She asked.

"You have always been thirty-nine. That is what you have told me all these years. I am round, fat, and fifty. Who cares how old someone our age is." He laughed. "After the public relations man gets his photo and our surprise engagement information, go type us up a pre-nuptial contract and a contract making you president. Be prepared to go down town to the courthouse first thing in the morning. We will be married by the Justice of the Peace when the courthouse opens."

"Ward, would you mind if I brought my mother from the nursing home. I feel like I have always been a source of shame to her and my Rabbi father. She only has two or three months to live. I would like her to see me do something that she could be proud of. You know how it is in the Jewish faith with the Sodom and Gomorrah thing."

"It is not a problem. I will even call her mother and hug her and kiss her if it will give you a little prestige in her eyes. My mother wanted me to be a doctor. I was a disappointment to her and my father. Dad never saw me as a successful banker. I am, but he never saw it." Ward replied.

"You are okay, Ward." She replied.

"Here is my credit card. Call and find us a photographer for in the morning. We will want six or eight photos for press releases, etc. After work, run out to the mall and pick yourself out a white suit and pick up some sort of flower bouquet thing to carry in the morning. Ask Callie to stand up with you. Buy her a dress of some sort that is bridesmaid appropriate. Keep this totally on the hush. I don't want any of our regular employees knowing anything about it till after we have officially tied the knot. I have got to get a divorce attorney for William and you installed as president before Betty finds out."

"One white suit, a photographer, a dress for Callie, and one pair of zipped lips, I've got it sir."

"Call and move my plane reservation for Hawaii till tomorrow. My two weeks at the Hawaiian fat farm and starvation center is a must. I can't do the office bit anymore, Madge. The doctor has laid down strict guidelines for my health if I want to live to be an old man."

"Don't worry about the Park Street Bank. I intend to give it my all and retire a legend. Thank you for this opportunity. It will end my working career in style."

"I hope to come home from Hawaii in better shape physically. However, I am not returning to the bank. You will run the show. What you say goes. For now, I want you to take two weeks off and not come in to the bank. Everyone will assume you are with me on a honeymoon. Take that credit card of mine and use it for anything you need. Take Callie and drive to the coast somewhere out of sight and enjoy a couple weeks with her. That card is good for twenty thousand. The pin is my birth year."

"You are one smart man, Ward. My hat is off to you on this one. I thought your father pulled off some major coups, you have topped him and managed to get around his trust."

A knock came at the door." Smile, Madge and pretend that you are crazy about me. Hang on me little bit. We are going to be the talk of the coffee shop tomorrow. Our engagement should come out in the morning paper."

"Won't the public relations man let this leak before morning?"

"Not if he wants to keep his job. I have already sworn him to secrecy and threatened his position on the phone. He is agreeable."

"I am going to ask that snooty coffee shop waitress for your table for the next three years. She sees secretaries, receptionists, and lesbians as peons and has treated me that way over the years."

"Enjoy my table and your revenge." He replied glancing at his hand. "Damn, I almost forgot. You better pick us up a couple cheap wedding bands, something that we can throw away and not feel guilty about three years from now. "

"If you don't mind, I think I would like to use my mother's rings. She has already given them to me and I think it would please her."

"Not a bad idea. Take this key and get into my lock box and find my dad's wedding band. It will save you one stop tonight."

"Well, at least I don't have to worry about a wedding night," she laughed.

"I am hoping that if I lose weight and get my sugar under control I might be able to function again. I really want a life with this woman that I have met. I know that she is the one for me. I am praying that the fat farm works and that I will be able to be intimate with her. I will introduce you to her when the hype dies down. I think you will like her. She comes from the other side of the tracks and doesn't know that I am rich or aware that I am a banker. She thinks that I am an out of work salesman. I keep our relationship beyond the tracks. Three years from now, you can divorce me on the grounds of adultery if you want. I might enjoy a little reputation of being a Romeo." He laughed.

The public relations director showed up with his camera and was shocked to the core when they shared their engagement with him. Ten minutes was all it took for him to take his photo and get the information he needed for the press release. Madge returned to her desk to type up two contracts grinning from ear to ear. Her mother would be proud of her. She was marrying a bank president. She would go out to the nursing home later and tell her. Her mother could die in peace knowing or thinking that her daughter was a good straight Jewish girl and had married well.

CHAPTER THIRTEEN

Ward Shows the Tape to William

About ten minutes after Madge and the Public relations manager left Ward's office, one by one three individuals made their way to his office. One was the bank security guard. The second was the Officer from the security firm that monitored the cameras and doors of the bank. Last to arrive was William looking worried.

"William, this is Jack Jarvis from the company that services our bank's cameras and monitors. He has pulled a tape for you to take a look at. I asked him here so that you wouldn't think that the tape was something I created. He watched the incident live when it was happening."

William shook hands with the man from the security firm."Has one of my employees out at the branch been caught doing something illegal?" he asked not really understanding why a security man needed to be there.

"We will get to that in a moment. You know Parker our security guard?"

"Yes, I know him."

"He is here, should you have a problem with what you are about to see. I want to tell you to begin with that I have met a girl and I am seriously thinking of marrying her. What you are going to see on this tape was not encouraged or invoked by me. This seduction was not of my doing in anyway."

"Don't tell me Marilyn Jenkins has made a pass at you. She is a good teller out at the branch who just happens to have a crush on you. For God's sake Ward, she is fifty and an old maid. You have no reason to fear her. She likes you. I thought we had a major problem with Stewart being fired. If it is Marilyn, I will have a talk with her."

The security man glanced at the security guard and bit his lip. Both did a shuffling of their feet.

"Sit down, William. Play the tape, boys." Ward stated in an uneasy voice. He was not sure what William's reaction would be.

First William saw Betty and his little boy Thomas standing just inside the back door carrying their retirement gift for Ward. Then he saw Ward enter and Betty send the boy off to the lobby to play. All the blood drained from his face as the three minute tape played out and he heard all the degrading remarks that issued from Betty's mouth about him and the children. His eyes filled with tears when he heard her ask Ward to join her in France and that they would forget that he and the children ever existed. He listened as Thomas returned and Ward scolded her for making such remarks in front of her child. Then the tape went blank.

"I am sorry, William. I came in the back door to avoid her, not meet her. You can ask my secretary. Her calloused words about you and your children must be a shock! God as my witness, William, I did not in any way seek out Betty or hatch this up. I will pay for you a divorce attorney. You need to beat her to the punch or she is going to leave you and the children high and dry. Do you understand what I am saying to you? "

Catching his breath and white as a sheet, William replied. "I understand very well. You couldn't be a sport and let Betty and I be happy. I fully believe the tape is authentic. However, I am sure you offered her who knows what to abandon me and the children. You can take your offer of an attorney and shove it up where the sun doesn't shine. I quit. The children and I don't need you. I have connections in the community and I am perfectly capable of getting another job. I bet you have planned this for fifteen years. I hope you are real happy with yourself. You have cost my children a mother."He then rose to his feet and walked out white as a sheet, teary eyed, and trembling.

Ward saw William as a fool. William saw Ward as jealous.

51

CHAPTER FOURTEEN

Ward Doesn't Call

Two weeks passed. Tattootie hadn't heard from her new friend, Ward Goldman. She really thought a man should make the first call. She didn't want to appear to be a needy female who jumped at any chance to have a man, any man in her life to lean on. However, she wondered why he hadn't called. He had said he would. She was lonely and had really hoped their time together would foster a friendship or possibly more.

She was tired of being seen as a freak. She longed for a normal world. She had hoped that normal world would include Ward. She had fantasized about dinner and movie dates with him and Saturday morning jogs together. She had seen herself having his children, a bunch of little butterballs that looked just like him. She didn't mind that he was heavy. To her disappointment, he didn't call. All her fantasies had to be trashed. She was pissed at herself for having believed that he was a possibility. A tear rolled down her cheek as she told herself that she had broken her rule. Don't get attached to anyone till you have known them for at least three months. Her rule always worked. She had no friends because the rule worked. "Never again!" she muttered.

It had been two weeks and the ball point pen tattoos had disappeared from her skin. She hadn't worn makeup since she was sixteen because of her face being a billboard. Now it was time to become a normal woman and enjoy some of the things that other women her age took for granted. She was going to experiment and reinvent herself. As a foster child, she wore rags and other people's hand me downs. As a tattoo model she wore halter tops and short shorts. Every inch of her exposed skin had been a chance to make money. Now her foster days and her tattoo model days were over. She was going to explore and create a non freak Tootie. She wasn't sure who that person was. She had always refused to give in to her desires for frivolities like makeup. Every penny she had made in the past had a planned destination toward her college degree. She had put all her personal wants aside in lieu of a better life for herself in the long run. She had always been nobody. She was looking forward to being somebody. She wished that Ward had seen her as someone. He was a big disappointment to her.

Today was the first day that her body was starting to look normal. The rash was gone and the tattoos had faded. She was secretly thrilled at the possibility of appearing pretty instead of a freak. However, she would never forget how the normal population, like the woman in the bank, treated her when she needed to be a freak to survive. She would choose her friends wisely.

Just as she was about to walk out the door, her phone rang. It was James from the tattoo parlor.

"Hey, girl, where have you been keeping yourself?" he asked.

"Indoors and wearing as little as possible to let my skin heal. That allergy rash was one miserable, itchy mess."

"Are you making it alright, financially? I know that you pretty much have lived from paycheck to paycheck putting yourself thru college."

"I will survive. I am going out into the normal world and seek employment today .My face has cleared up and I am going to give it a try. It is time to reinvent myself again. What are you up to?"

"For starters, that loan banker of yours is in the morning paper. It seems that he and his wife have just returned from a two week honeymoon in Hawaii. Did you say he was a heavy dude?"

"The man I met on the bus bench was heavy and his name was Ward Goldman. The loan officer's name was Stewart. What does it say about the loan officer?

"I will read you the photo caption and save the clipping if you want me to. Here it goes, Ward Goldman, president and owner of the Park Street Bank has returned from a two week honeymoon in Hawaii. His wife, Madge, will be taking over as president of the financial institution. "He replied stopping to sneeze."Sorry about that, Tootie. My allergies are acting up."

"What else does it say about Ward Goldman?" she asked sure that there must be two Wards.

"It just goes on with some banking jive announcing Mrs. Goldman's position as bank president".

"Save the article for me James. It doesn't sound like the loan officer I encountered. I do recall the name plaque on his desk reading Stewart. Maybe his last name was Steward and he goes by Ward. Save the clipping and I will put it on my dart board."

"I might throw a couple darts at him myself. From what you have told me, he is a real asshole."

"Asshole is a minor word to use describing him. Asshole is a compliment." She replied.

James laughed and then continued. "Some man keeps calling and leaving his phone number for you at the tattoo parlor. We tell him that you don't work for us anymore and that we don't give out addresses and telephone numbers. We figure he is one of our clients and obsessed with you for some reason. He seems to know all about our business. I think he may be a possible stalker. Do you want us to give him your number? I think he said his name was Ed something or another."

"No, he is probably one of those perverts that hang out in the shop. One offered me money awhile back thinking I was a call girl. Needless to say, I set him straight."She replied. "What else is on your mind?"

"I hate the tattoo business and I have decided to tell my dad so. I have saved my money and have enough for the down payment on a truck related business venture. "He replied.

"That sounds exciting," she stated wanting to sound supportive.

"How about meeting me at Pete's café just?" he asked. The café was a few doors down from his father's tattoo shop. "I will bring you the news article and buy you a burger."

"Free food," she replied. "You know how I feel about anything free. I am a survivor and a free meal helps this starving college student survive one more day. I will need to catch the bus over. How does an hour sound?"

"One hour it is."He replied and then hung up.

CHAPTER FIFTEEN

Tears and a Burger

Tootie reached Pete's café first. She went in and claimed them a back booth where they could talk privately. She was really curious about the news paper clipping. She glanced over to the counter where a waitress was idly filling salt shakers.

"There wouldn't be a copy of this morning's paper in here anywhere?" she asked. "Perhaps one that someone has left behind."

"There sure is. A customer left one behind. I was taking a peek earlier at the sale ads in it." She said retrieving a folded up disorganized mess of a paper from under the counter. "Don't take the coupons, I want them."

"I am just interested in reading an article about a loan officer from the bank where I do business."

"It is on the social page. I read it because I recognized his wife's picture. She used to come in her with a friend. I always thought she was a lesbian. I guess I was wrong about that. She has married that fat banker they call Ward Goldman. He is one of the richest men in town."

Tootie thumbed thru the paper thinking that she was going to spot a photo of her jerk loan officer and his new bride. When she finally found the page due to the pages of the paper all being out of order, she gasped. Then she started trembling and her eyes filled with tears. Her bus bench Ward Goldman was the bank president Ward Goldman. While she had been waiting for him to call, he was on the beach in Hawaii with his new wife. She had been used for some sort of cheap thrill by him. He was engaged the day he took her for coffee and asked for her phone number. He must have seen her as some cheap tattoo trash coffee time entertainment. She burst into tears. After a couple minutes of staring at his photo and the woman that was his wife, she closed the paper and wiped her tears away with a white restaurant napkin.

Jo Hammers

Then she got up and handed the paper back to the waitress thanking her.

Tootie hugged her hot mug of coffee and tried to control her emotions. "Never again, Tootie, You will never share yourself with another normal man ever again. Never again," she muttered to herself. "You should have known he was a jerk just like all of the other normal snobs in society. He was not interested in you! You were some sort of cheap afternoon thrill. Have coffee with the tattoo girl before you tie the knot. He saw you as some cheap stripper type that normally shows up at bachelor parties. Only you were at a bachelor party for two. He used you for a cheap last minute thrill before getting married."

She gave her eyes and nose a good wiping. She could see thru the window James getting out of his old pickup. She would never be able to tell anyone about her folly. She was embarrassed to the core and wouldn't want anyone to know that she had been so easily used. She had waited two weeks for him to call while he was married

CHAPTER SIXTEEN

James Makes an Offer

" Suck it up, Tootie.""She said to herself as she watched thru the window James exit his pickup." You are your own best friend. Now it is time to be that friend and get focused. You were temporarily sideswiped by a normal man. You have learned your lesson and now it is time to watch out for yourself. No one is going to watch out for. You have got to create a world for yourself and then rule it. That world does not include Ward Goldman. He is history. Now suck it up and quit making a fool out of yourself crying."

James entered smiling and slid into the booth across from her and ordered a cup of coffee from the waitress.

Tootie forced herself to smile and asked, "Bend my ear. Tell me about your new business idea."

"For starters, I walked right off and left that newspaper clipping."

"Forget about that. I moved my checking account the day they turned me down for a loan. The Park Street Bank is history. I need to establish a business relationship with a bank that will be there for me. One more semester and I have my degree in business. I am going to start a business. I just haven't decided what kind yet."

"That is what I want to talk to you about. I need a business partner that I can trust. After working with you for the last five years, I know that you are about as honest as they come and that your college education has given you the business head that I need. Are you open to hearing a business venture idea for two?"

"Sure, lay it on me. I seem to be in a brain fog right now. What do you have in mind?"

"Have you seen noticed those big dumpsters that the trash companies deliver to construction sites? They are also used where houses are being torn down or re-modeled."

"Yes, I am familiar with them. Why?"

"Those dumpsters bring in two hundred dollars a day plus the cost of dumping them. The Westside bank has repossessed six of them plus the truck that delivers them. They just put them up for sale this week. The deal comes with one small commercial lot and a shack on it. They were turned over to the bank by some widow whose husband up and died suddenly. She was not interested in the business and had no boys to take it over. Anyway, if you and I could purchase keep those six dumpsters in use, I think that you and I could possibly make six hundred a week each and make the loan payment. It wouldn't be like working eight hours a day. We might have to pickup, dump, and deliver one or two dumpsters a day. You could take the late day ones to work around your college schedule and I would take the morning runs plus truck the full ones to the landfill to dump them. You could do the books."

"That much money would cover my next semester of college expenses and feed me! However, have you forgotten that I don't have a commercial driver's license or haven't driven a car in three years?" she replied in a voice that said she was a little shocked at his consideration of her.

"Truck driving school is just about six weeks of training and then you sign on with a company and they put you out on the road for a ninety day try out. If you signed up and attended January classes, I would have the company up and running by the time you got out. You could sign on into your own company for the training period. " He stated filling her in on the details."

"Number one, I don't have the finances to pay for truck driving school and number two, my final semester of college classes starts in January."

"I hate to ask this, would you consider skipping one semester of college? You could enter the summer session to finish up and graduate. It wouldn't be like you were dropping out. You will just be adding a different type of education to your portfolio. Truck driving women don't put up with any crap off of anyone. You have that air about you. I will pay your tuition to truck driving school and your rent for two months if you will sign a contract with me becoming my partner."

"What do these dumpster deliverers wear, anyway? I was hoping to move up a little bit in society and wear a little makeup and run an office somewhere till I started a business of my own."

"They wear Jeans, boots, and ball caps like the male drivers do. After the first year, you could run the office and we could hire one Jackass to drive in your place and work him eight hours a day taking over your deliveries and mine. At that point, we could pick up a second used truck somewhere and add another six dumpsters to our business inventory. Every year we could add one truck and six dumpsters till you and I are making a comfortable living. Once a year, we will split the profits three ways. You and I will take a third and the other third we will put back in to the company. Plus, you and I will take out a weekly wage just as though we were employees. Does that sound reasonable? We could be good together. As the business grows, I will run the rough everyday end of the business and you can be the big wig CEO in the office chair. I am not interested in the office scene. I want to be free, out and about?"

"I will agree to it if we have a legal partnership agreement drawn up by an attorney. I am no dummy and I won't be used." She replied cringing knowing that she was going to become a dumpster queen. She just wouldn't tell her friends in suburbia how she made her money. She would leave home in the morning in heels and put on the coveralls after getting to work. It wasn't that she looked down on those in the garbage and dumpster business, it was that she didn't want to be seen as a freak anymore. She wanted friends."

"I am sure that I can have an attorney draw up the partnership papers in two or three days." He replied."I will give you a call and tell you where to meet me to sign them."

"I will be there." She stated.

"I have got to run now that I know you are willing. I think that I have time to get in with an attorney friend of mine before closing if I hurry. He is older and just works part of a day. Do you mind eating lunch alone? Here is a ten. Get yourself a burger and do a little brainstorming while you sit here on ideas to make our little venture successful."

With that said, James slid back out of the booth leaving her to eat alone. He stopped to say a few words to the salt shaker filling waitress whom he knew. Then he was gone.

Tootie relaxed in the booth and ordered herself a burger and fries and muttered to herself as she was eating. "The universe has brought to you your next step in life. Go with the flow, Tootie, and see where it takes you."

CHAPTER SEVENTEEN

The Shack

Tootie closed her account with the Park Street Bank and gave them no forwarding address. She then moved out of her apartment the next day and in with James while she went to trucking school to save rent and utility money. James had offered to pay her rent, but she told him that they needed to save every penny he had to get the business up and running. Secretly cringing, she dropped out of college for one semester. She wasn't a person who dropped out of anything. She was a goal setter and a nose to the grind stone type of person. However, when she aced truck driver training she felt good about the fact that she would always have a second occupation to fall back on that paid good money if she ever had need of it.

Tattootie disappeared into the world beyond the tracks on the wrong side of the city abandoning all   past connections and leaving no forwarding address. She entered an anti social faze of her life. Ward did a number on her self esteem. She felt dirty like he had seen her as some low class streetwalker that he wanted to toy with as a little diversion on the afternoon before his wedding. She no longer saw herself as a woman that a normal man would want. Ward burst that bubble real good. She decided it was probably in the stars for her to die old and alone. She had trusted him and spent two hours spilling her guts out to him. She now saw normal men as untrustworthy creeps who only wanted to use women from the other side of the tracks. She returned to her imaginary lover William who had been there for her for years. He didn't break her heart and she liked the way he looked in her pink bath towel in the mornings. She knew he wasn't real, but she needed imaginary him to survive. Ward ended her dream of a normal man from the suburbs who would want her. She was disillusioned. She was Tattootie, a woman that no one wanted. So, she turned to William. He was safe.

Once the partnership papers were signed, it was a whirlwind year of trucks, dumpsters, and finishing up her college year in the summer session. James was right. The dumpster business provided them both with around five hundred dollars a week to begin with. After two or three months she once again rented herself a cheap apartment and saved every penny possible to put herself thru her final semester of college. She graduated after the summer session.

By fall, the business was steady and Tattootie was saving money. She no longer had college expenses to pay for, so it was time to move forward and set a new goal. The down payment on the house she had dreamed of her whole life was next. James seemed content living in his apartment, but Tootie was not. She had come up with a new idea to help her get where she wanted to go. When James returned from a landfill run, she yelled for him to come to the shack of an office. It basically was two dilapidated rooms and a bathroom. They hadn't done anything to it except install their phone line and put in a desk and computer system for the business. Their customers all placed their orders by phone. So, the office and its lack of paint and weak floors were as not important.

"What is up?" he asked stepping inside and removing his ball cap, a courtesy that Tootie insisted on."I have a strange request that I need your okay for." She replied hanging up the phone. She had been on it taking an order.

"Lay it on me, I am in a hurry. I have a full afternoon of dumpster deliveries".

"I want to give up my apartment and save all of my earnings for the down payment on a house in the suburbs. You know that has been my one goal for years."

"Where do you plan on living?" he asked quickly wanting her to get to the point.

"I would like to sell off all of my things and put up a twin bed back there in the storage room. If I could survive here in the office rent free for the next year, I could buy that house I want. Would that be agreeable? I know you have a lot of our business crap back there. I thought we could buy one of those cheap wooden sheds, have it delivered, and move the tools etc. in it." She replied.

"Oh crap, Tootie. I can't let you live out here on the rough side of town alone in this flea bitten rat trap of a building."

"I have lived in worse, James. In case you have forgotten, I lived on top of a laundry building exposed to the elements for a year when I first ran away from foster care."

"I guess this is the Ritz compared to that. Okay, it is alright with me as long as you get a big, mean, vicious dog and keep it in inside with you at night. There are transients and men out of work living in the alleys and on the streets in this neighborhood." He replied shaking his head.

"I know. There have been a few drop in here and ask for work," she replied pushing a button to put an incoming phone call on hold.

"You do know that Mrs. Rosamond, next door, feeds the bums. She is going to get herself murdered. I don't want you ending up a victim with her."

"Maybe it would be a good thing, my living here. I could share my vicious, mean dog with her," replied Tootie smugly.

"Women . . .! You don't have a lick of sense." He replied shaking his head. "If you are intent on doing this, I will load that small magnum of mine. It is small enough that you can keep in your pocket. I want you to sleep with it in your pajamas as well."

"And what if I don't wear pajamas?" she asked to annoy him.

"That is a little more than I want to know, thank you. Put the gun at night where you will as long as it is in bed with you. Promise me!"

"It's a deal." She replied.

"I have been meaning to tell you that there is some young guy sleeping just beyond the back of our property in that abandoned semi tractor. Make sure you keep the office doors locked when you are here alone."

"I am a street kid, remember? I know the score! You don't have to worry about me."

"It has been a good year, Tootie. On the first day of January we will take our third of the profit. From what I can tell from the books, you and I are going to have about thirty thousand a piece. What are you going to do with your share?" he asked.

"I plan to work on my master's degree. What I don't need for that, I will put in my house down payment fund."

"I was thinking of a little trip to Vegas on mine."

"You really need to consider what you want out of life, James. You need to set yourself some goals. Gambling, women, motorcycles, toy trucks, and seeing how fast you can drive our container trucks without getting a ticket should be replaced with some serious plans for your future. That thirty thousand could make you a down payment on a condo or another small business of some sort. Give it some thought."

"You know me better than anyone, Tootie. I don't know what I would do without you." He replied bowing to her. Rising from his theatrical position, he added. "We need to talk about hiring our first employee. The office and phones are starting to eat up your time. We need to take a step forward and buy two more trucks and more dumpsters. Will you take a look at the books, give it some thought, and then give me your opinion. I trust your judgment."

"I don't have to look. We are at the point we are going to have to do some hiring plus make some equipment purchases. We will talk about it when you finish this afternoon. I will put together a business plan for the next year and have it ready to show you."

"I am glad you agree with me," he replied.

"The phone has rung off the hook this morning. Living here, our missed calls alone would probably pay for the new guy and a third truck. If I was answering the phone sixteen hours a day, six days a week, our business could probably double and maybe triple. I am willing to shop and socialize on Sundays only if you are willing to put in a six day, ten hours a day driving.

"That is what I like about you, Tootie. You are a no-non-sense woman who keeps me chained to my steering wheel. We are a good team. However, every girl I date thinks we have something going on. They usually end up dumping me because I won't get rid of you. I am too embarrassed to tell them that you are the brains of this operation and if anyone had to go, it would be me. When they get inquisitive about you, I dump them to save face. You are one smart cookie, but hard on my love life. Why do you have to be so dam beautiful? The women in my life see you as a threat."

"No one should choose their friends or companions because of looks. "When I was a freak tattoo model, no one wanted to be friends with me. The gorgeous girls you date are the back stabbing types who used to give me a hard time when I was trying to survive. Forgive me, but I enjoy watching them squirm. I don't need snobbish idiots in my life like those you date. I have given up on having friends or a knight in shining armor. I have one important goal, a home."

"At least you have a home as a goal. I am not sure what I want out of life. I do know that I have always wanted to be a truck driver. I am halfway living that dream. Sometimes, I get that old itch to want to see the country from the window of a semi. Do we ever get what we truly want?"

"We are our own paintbrushes, James. If we want something to happen in life, we have to make it happen. If I want a house, I have to make it happen. Whatever it is that you want, you have to take out your paintbrush, paint yourself a picture in your mind, and then work towards that goal. There are no free rides in life".

"So, I should take my love of trucking to the next level?"

"Climbing one rung of your personal ladder at a time is how you become what you want to be. I ate tuna from a can and peanut butter for years as I climbed my ladder to be an educated woman. Even now, I am setting new goals to conquer."

"You are right, Tootie. I am living half a dream. Even as successful as our business venture is, my father thinks I am living substandard. Women hate what I do for an occupation. My mother, bless her soul, tells me she is ashamed to tell her friends that her son is a garbage man. However, I personally, think the two of us have done quite well for ourselves. Both of us are paying our rent and our bills. You have a new car and I have a new four wheel drive. I think we have done pretty well for our first year of being in business."

"My current goals are a home and a master's degree. You have to decide what you want from your life experience."

"I will give it some thought," he replied putting on his ball cap and turning to leave the office. He turned back to her for a brief moment and said."I will help you move over the holidays when you are ready."

Christmas came and went. Tootie moved in to the two room shack they called an office and prepared to rough it for a year in order to save money for the down payment on a house in the suburbs

CHAPTER EIGHTEEN

Mrs. Rosamond

A couple evenings after she moved into the two room shack of an office, a knock came on the door one evening. James was gone. She hadn't found a mean dog yet, so she was cautious and inquired who was there before opening it.

"It is your neighbor, Mrs. Rosamond from next door. You purchased your business from me and the bank."

Tootie grinned and opened the door. "You and the bank have been very good to me. What can I do for you?" she asked amused at the seventyish little Jewish woman. The business had been a bank repo.

"I have never bothered you during the day because I know you have a business to run. Now that you are here at night, I thought we might become lady friends. We are the only two women living here in this maze of trash and trucking businesses."

"I think that might be a possibility," Tootie replied. "We do live in a man's world here."

"Your office was my first home when I came here from Hungary. We built it from scrap lumber found in our dumpsters. We would pull all of the construction supplies before we took the dumpsters to the land fill. There is love and dreams in every board. We had nothing but one truck, six dumpsters, this lot, and a huge mortgage. There was no money for a home. We had to be creative and use what we could come up with. We lived in a dumpster turned on its side to begin with. We stretched a painter's tarp over the open side. My husband and I were very happy in our dumpster home."

"You and I have a lot in common, Mrs. Rosamond. Would you like to come in?" Tootie asked.

Jo Hammers

The elderly Jewish looking old woman stepped inside and then continued her conversation."My purpose in visiting with you is to make you aware that a young stranger is living in the old abandoned semi truck cab behind us. I have been feeding him breakfast every morning. He was a banker till he lost his job a year ago."

"I will lock my door and windows," replied Tootie. "You should not let him inside your house. Street people will lie to you about who they once were. They will steal from you when they get a chance."

"I am a good judge of character. He is telling the truth. He says that a devil woman got him fired. He hasn't been able to find another position. He has lost his car and apartment. It is a long way from Park Place to down here .The slippery slide got him. I am sure that he was probably living beyond his means and didn't expect to get fired. Do you think you might possibly have a job of some sort open? He could walk to work from where he is living. That is a good thing." She laughed.

"Tell him to approach James. He does the hiring. If he legitimately wants to work, we might be able to use him. He would be on a ninety day trial basis and have to work for minimum wage." She replied.

"That is great. He knows how to invest money. He will take your minimum wage and make himself rich. He has a business plan made and will move up in the world. He wants to rub his success in the face of his rich uncle who fired him."

"I like a person that has goals. Have him see James."

I will send him over to speak with James after he eats breakfast with me in the morning. I am serving fried mush tomorrow morning with honey on it. He eats what I eat." Mrs. Rosamond giggled. "I am sure he didn't eat mush where he has come from. He says someday, when he has money again, he will take me downtown to the Park Street Bistro for breakfast and we will eat corn beef hash and eggs with sourdough toast."

"Don't plan on it, Mrs. Rosamond. He is using you for a free ride." Tootie replied."Street people will promise you anything to get fed or money for drugs and alcohol."

"There are no free rides in my house, Miss Tootie. My husband and I worked for every meal we had. I make my breakfast companion do the dishes if he wishes to eat with me. He didn't even know how to run a sink of dish water when I first met him. He does pretty well now. Although, he uses way too much dish liquid. I don't say anything. He is learning to be a man who can take care of himself. A good man is able to clean up after himself."

"I like you! I am a no free rides person, myself. Making him do dishes for his food pleases me. Does he get the dishes clean?" she asked giggling.

"Oh yes! If he doesn't, I make him redo them. Stewart likes to eat and he knows the rules."

"So you are on a first name basis with him?" she asked.

"He must call me Mrs. Rosamond. That is respectful. However, he is servant status. I am entitled to call him by his first name. He is a Jew like me. His biggest flaw is his hatred of women. I tell him that a good Jew must love his enemy. I tell him to love his devil woman and then beat the pants off of her in a business deal and take all of her money to get even."

Tootie choked back a laugh. The little woman was witty. "What is his name, in case he shows up here in the office looking for work?"

"Stewart Goldman." She replied.

Tootie gasped. It couldn't be the loan officer that she had been verbally attacked by. She would have James check him out

"Be careful, Mrs. Rosamond. Your breakfast companion may have stolen someone's identity. He could have a criminal record."

"He is genuine. I checked him out. I went down to the Park Street Bank and asked about him. He worked there. One of the tellers told me about him. He was a rich little asshole that they all hated. I like taming assholes. My husband was one. I made a man out of him. I will do the same to the little banker ass hole living out back.

"I love you, Mrs. Rosamond. Men don't walk on you, do they?"

"A woman must keep her cold feet always in the back of a man so he won't forget that she is there. You should never let a man be comfortable enough to walk on you."

"I agree. A little over a year ago I met a man and opened myself up to him like a book. He read me and then discarded me. The only thing now that a man will ever get from me is my cold feet in his back." Tootie replied remembering her experience with Ward.

"I do hope you forgive me for asking a favor. I am an old woman with no children. I cannot ask Stewart for this favor. I have an itchy spot on my left upper hip. I can't see what the problem is. Would it be an imposition to ask you to peek at it and tell me if it looks like cancer? My husband had skin cancers. I am afraid I might have caught one from him."

Tootie started to laugh, but quickly caught herself. She bit her lip in amusement. The little woman was serious.

"Skin cancers are caused by the sun or chemicals. You can't catch them from another person. However, I will be happy to take a peek if it will set your mind at ease." Tootie replied amused.

"Thank you, thank you....." Mrs. Rosamond replied and turned around with her backside to Tootie. She then lifted her blouse and pulled down the elastic waist of her old lady pants for Tootie to look.

"You don't have to worry. You just have a bad pimple on your hip like it is the eye of your butterfly. It will be sore a couple days and then go away. Have you been hitting the chocolate bars?" That was what her social worker used to ask her when she was a pimply teen and still in foster care. She was surprised that the seventyish old lady had a butterfly tattoo on her hip. However, she didn't pursue the subject of the tattoo.

"You must be psychic. I ate two today. Is the other world telling me to give up chocolate? In Hungary we had witches who saw between worlds. I was told to get a butterfly tattoo when I got to America and I would fly high on love."

"So, that is why you have a butterfly tattoo on your hip? A witch told you to get one?"

"Yes. It is a sign between me and the world beyond that I believe in psychics, witches, and fortune tellers."

"If I had tattoos all over my body, would you see me as a tattooed friend or as a tattooed foe?" Tootie asked fishing. She still saw herself as she once was, a rejected woman by normal people. Now she judged people by that experience.

"Neither, you would have to be a saint or a goddess. I thought I was going to die from the needles when that butterfly was put on. I can't imagine the pain of someone having their whole body done. My heart would break seeing my friend in pain. I cried when I got my butterfly. I would cry with you. Then I would be happy with you that you had something that was meaningful to you."

Tootie grinned. This little woman said what she thought and had an interesting way of putting things.

"If I should want my whole body covered with tattoos, would you go with me as a friend for support?" she asked one last time fishing to see if she should go down this road exploring a possible friendship. Ward was the last person that she opened herself up to and she had kicked herself a thousand times since then for trusting him. She had envisioned herself marrying him and growing old with him and her going first and dying in his arms. It had been over a year. She wasn't opening herself up to another disappointment.

"I would do more than go with you. I would go light a candle for you on my husband's grave and ask him to put in a good word for you with Father Abraham in case you were killed by the thousands of needles. I would tell him that you were a modern day Joseph putting on a skin coat of many colors. I would ask him to guard you from above, if he made it there?"

"You would share with me your husband's attention from the other side?"

"You would need a guardian angel. When you have a coat of many colors, those about you would want to sell you off into slavery because you are special. A full skin coat of many colors would be a sign that God has chosen you to be different, not a cookie cutter human. Men would desire your coat! Evil humans might skin you for it. If you had a skin coat of many colors, I would have to get out my sewing machine and make you a full body suit to hide your specialness. I have to keep my butterfly hidden. If I let it show, all the old men in their many trucks whizzing by my house stop and want my skin, my specialness. It is hard being special. It is easy for humans to be cookie cutter images of each other. I am special and so are you. However, sometimes we must live lonely lives with no friends because we have goals and reasons for our specialness. I am beautiful with my butterfly tattoo. Men want me. I must keep my butterfly hidden till I find a man that I want. A cookie cutter man won't do."

Tootie broke out into laughter. "We will have to be careful with our butterflies, won't we?"

Mrs. Rosamond was sent by those beyond the grave to be Tootie's first real friend.

CHAPTER NINETEEN

Stewart Asks for a Job

It was a bitter cold morning. Tootie put a filter and coffee into their 1950's old fashioned chrome percolator and turned it on. She had found the old coffee maker on a shelf in the back when they first opened for business. They had agreed to purchase nothing that wasn't necessary. They were in business to make money, not spend it. The coffee pot worked, so they used it. As the antiquated pot whistled   and moaned, the smell of hot black coffee permeated the air making the cold, drafty shack they called an office tolerable.

Tootie was wearing a hooded university logo sweatshirt, jeans, and her driving boots. On her head was a long blonde wig, On top of the wig, she wore her worn old stocking hat. The wig plus the stocking hat kept her head warm in the drafty office. James teased her sometimes about the wig. He preferred her dark short hair. She had cut her long dark ponytail shortly after meeting Ward. She had told herself that the ponytail made her look like she was a child. Ward not calling had pushed her out of her last bit of childish belief that there was someone out there that would love her. With the ritual cutting of her hair, she became a woman who knew she only had herself to depend on. She threw her knight in shining armor fantasy in the trash can along with the shorn long locks of dark brown hair. James never said a thing about her missing locks. She was glad. However, the blonde wig drove him crazy. He made lots of comments about it. Yesterday, he had asked her if she was going thru a blonde bimbo stage. She told him to get out of her office if he didn't like the fashion look for the day. The wig was purely a comfort item. The office was icy at times. She was sure that it had no insulation in the walls. The wig plus the stocking hat kept her head and ears warm. Sometimes she had to wear gloves inside the office with the fingers cut out to answer the phone. There were no frills such as a constant temperature in the Office.

As Tootie was pouring a mug of the hot brewed coffee, James entered in a hurry and grabbed his clipboard from the desk with his schedule for pickups and deliveries. He had been catching himself going and coming for weeks. He paused in front of the desk where Tootie had sat down with her coffee before tackling the business end of the day.

"Tootie, we have got to hire some help. I have reached the limit of what I can do in a day. Have we had anyone apply for a job? They had an ad running in the help wanted column of the local paper."

"Not a single one, James. I guess being a driver for a trash dumpster business doesn't have much sex appeal." She laughed.

"I tell the ladies I meet that I am an environmental specialist. It sounds great and they don't know what the hell it means." He added laughing.

"Mrs. Rosamond told me that the young guy living out back across the fence is looking for work. I haven't had an opportunity to get a look at him. You might walk back there, get acquainted, and make an assessment to see if we could use him."

"All we need is two hands on the steering wheel. If he can drive, he is a possibility. I will walk back there later when I have a moment and check him out. If nothing else, he could answer the phones and you could drive. There is no money in the office to steal."

"Whatever it takes, James, to get us moving forward into our second year. I plan on making money for my house fund. If it means me driving and letting some wimp answer the phone, it is alright with me. We just won't leave anything lying around that he could make a dollar on. He is probably an addict or an alcoholic."

"We were once tattoo freaks, but the dumpster business saved us. Maybe it could do the same for him."

"I once was lost, but now I am found." She laughed waving him out of the office.

About three hours later, the office door opened and Mrs. Rosamond's Stewart entered and waited for Tootie to get off the phone.

Looking up, Tootie swallowed hard. It was the loan officer who had ridiculed her and called her a freak. In shock, she didn't say anything for a moment.

"May I help you?"

"I spoke with your driver, James. He said that you might be looking for some help. I would like to fill out an employment application."

Tootie realized that he didn't recognize her due to the long blonde wig she was wearing as well as her skin being free of tattoos. She was thankful. She didn't want her day spoiled by another altercation with him. However, she was happy that Karma had caught up with him. He was in her position now."

"What qualifications do you have that would be of interest to us?" she asked handing him a standard employment form that she had picked up at the office supply and stamped with their letter head.

"For five years, I worked as a loan officer for the Park Street Bank. I will be honest with you. They will not give me a reference. I was fired for theft. I had a cup from a golf club. They claimed I pilfered it. Any type of theft isn't tolerated by the Park Street Branch. The cup was actually given to me earlier in the day by the branch manager's wife. She takes little things like logo cups and glasses from restaurants. I was naïve enough to take it. I never considered it would be seen as theft. A woman wearing tattoos pointed it out and I got canned for it. The recession and unexpected circumstances afterward put me under."

"That is an interesting tale. You still haven't told me what you can offer us if we hire you. Can you drive a truck?"

"No, but I am willing to learn. I have driven all sorts of gear shift sports cars. Driving is driving. I am sure that I can catch on." He replied.

Tootie tried not to stare as he filled out the application. She so wanted to tell him to get out of her office and call him white trash like he had called her tattoo trash. She controlled herself. She knew what it was like to be kicked when you were down. She wouldn't do that to anyone, not even him. When he was done, he returned the application to her.

"I just spoke with James on his cell and he said to hire you on a trial basis. You will answer to him and tackle whatever job he assigns you. Each employee here does anything and everything. I may run this office in the morning and drive one of the trucks in the afternoon if we are swamped. We are a no frills company with no health insurance or other benefits. We live and breathe to keep the business afloat and growing. If you want to grow with us and climb up out of the poverty state you are in, you will find James to be a real friend. I on the other hand, live and breathe to keep James and now you so busy that you can't find a moment to grab a hamburger during the day. I am the company taskmaster. You will enter the office only to clock in and to collect your paycheck. Otherwise, the office is off limits to you unless James assigns you to answering the phone if I should need to drive. When I am in the office, I am too busy on the phones to fool with anyone wanting to talk or grab a cup of coffee. If you want to talk, chat with Mrs. Rosamond before you come to work. Bring your morning coffee with you. I don't make coffee for the hired help."

"I understand," he replied. "Thank you for giving me a chance. I desperately need this job."

"What do you plan on doing with your first pay check?"She asked."I will pay you on Friday since I know you need money. After that, you get paid every two weeks like James and I. If you squander your check on drugs and alcohol don't expect a loan against your pay check to tide you over. I am only paying you for what you work this week to be nice. One kind gesture is all you will get from me for the duration of your employment. There are no free rides in this life and I live by that saying."

"I totally understand. Mrs. Rosamond, next door, has been really kind to me. I would not have given her the time of day a year ago. Now, I see that wealth and being someone doesn't mean a mansion on the other side of town or a healthy bank account. Wealth is having someone like her willing to be your friend. I was a real asshole when I first met her. She has tamed me and loved me. I am spending my whole first paycheck on her. I am going to take her by taxi downtown to the Park Street Bistro for breakfast and stuff her with corn beef hash and eggs."

"Isn't the bistro near the Park Street Bank? I have never eaten there, but I have had coffee in the little coffee shop a couple doors from the bank."

"The bistro is a half a block down from the coffee shop." He replied.

"I had a great cup of coffee with a friend there once."

"My uncle, Ward Goldman, likes that place."

"I think I have heard that name somewhere. What does your uncle do?"She asked trying not to sound too curious.

"He owns the Park Street Bank. The day after he fired me, he married his secretary, and then flew off to Hawaii on a honeymoon like I meant nothing to him. I wasn't invited to his wedding and that really hurt. I don't ever remember a Christmas, Thanksgiving, or birthday without our celebrating it together. He discarded me like I was garbage. It is funny what little things stick in your mind that you associate with personal trauma. I remember his flight time for his honeymoon trip and a tattooed woman client. The rest of the day is a blur in my memory. "

Tootie wanted to cry. The two weeks that she had sat and waited for Ward to call her, he wasn't in the city. He was on a beach somewhere with his secretary. In their talk he never mentioned that he had a fiancé or was planning to marry the next day. She felt sick at her stomach. Ward had played a sick perverted game pretending to be her friend. She now had two Goldman men to hate and one was standing in front of her. It was all she could do to smile, hand Stewart a construction worker's orange vest and send him out the door to James. The company needed help and that over rode her need for revenge.

CHAPTER TWENTY

The Squirrel Skin Cap

Tootie had worn the blonde wig and stocking hat for weeks in an effort to keep her identity hidden from Stewart. He was working out and had aced his CDL driver's test. They needed him. The want ad for drivers had been a bomb. No one had called or dropped by to fill out an application. Stewart did take Mrs. Rosamond downtown for breakfast when he got his first small paycheck. She was thrilled and talked about her adventure with him for days. She went on and on about Stewart opening the doors for her and ordering for her. Stewart was filling a hole in Mrs. Rosamond's world. After the breakfast outing, she had a twinkle in her eye and Stewart to talk incessantly about. Tootie just listened. She was tolerating Stewart.

It was payday. James was first to the office at the end of the day to collect his paycheck. He had time to date again now that there was hired help. He was anxious to get his check and on the weekend road to love. Tootie handed him his check after signing it and tearing it from the company's check book.

"Don't spend this all in one place. You know the company rule, James. We don't make loans to hold you over till the next pay day." She stated digging him.

"You are a cold hearted taskmaster." He laughed taking his check. "That is why I chose to go in to business with you. With you at the company helm, I can't throw my assets away on wild women. I have to go for mild women because that is all I can afford."

"You will appreciate my whip when we you get your company dividend check in January. "She replied. "Last year it was thirty thousand. If business keeps picking up, it is possible that we will get forty-five or fifty this next go round."

"Tootie, you have been a great asset to me. However, could you take some money out of my share and replace that damn blonde wig you have been wearing for weeks. It is driving me crazy. It has to be the ugliest creature I have ever seen. I can't live another week having to look at that thing. Promise me you will throw the creepy creature in the trash this weekend. You are a dam beautiful woman. I just don't get the wig wearing faze you are going thru. Either you trash it, or I am going to sneak in here when you are asleep and take the thing and burn it. Blonde bimbo just doesn't suit you."

"It is that bad, huh?"

"Worse. Please take my handgun you carry and shoot the sucker."

"You know that I wear it and the stocking hat to keep my head warm. This office is like an iceberg at times."

"I will buy you one of those fur lined, ear flapped men's hunting caps. You can pull down the ear flaps when the office gets cold." He stated.

"It is a deal. However, I am not getting rid of the wig till the cap arrives."

"Stewart . . .!" shouted James.

Stewart entered carrying a small plastic bag from a farm supply and handed it to James grinning.

"Here you are. Stewart and I went halves on it. He would like to see the blonde creature on your head shot and put out of its misery also." James stated pulling a squirrel lined cap from the bag. He then proceeded to cut the plastic secured price tag off the hat and then handed it to her."We would rather have you look like us than a starved, escaped, yellow, mangy cat from the dog pound."

Caught off guard, Tootie took the hat and inspected its earmuffs and furry lining. "And just how many poor little squirrels lost their life so that I could have this marvel? She asked amused and feeling really good. She couldn't remember the last time anyone had given her a gift. Most women get flowers. To them she was a squirrel hat type of woman. That was alright. At least they had bought her a gift and secretly she loved it.

"Put it on," laughed Stewart. "We are going to cut your blonde creature in half and hang it from our radio antennae."

At that point, the pair of grinning men pulled new matching squirrel hats from their back pockets and put them on laughing.

"Alright, you get the blonde demon. However, you are not seeing me put the cap on. I will go in the bathroom where I can comb my hair and put it on properly. I don't want the two of you laughing at me when my real hair is all a mess."

"No way, stated James and he made a lunge and pulled off the stocking hat and blonde wig with one swoop of his long arm.

Tootie squealed and grabbed her head fluffing her short dark hair. "You have had it James. You just wait. The next time you have a serious relationship going, I am going to your new love that you are a cross dresser and own a blonde wig!" she yelled giggling like a school girl."Wipe that grin off of your face Stewart. You are already on my list." She stated and then realized what she had just said. She bit her lip and quickly put the hat on turning from them to regain her composure. Then she turned back to them and said, "Thank You. The hat is the nicest gift anyone has given me in a long time. I will cherish it."

"We have conquered the wearer of the blonde creature," laughed James who quickly left. He had two more deliveries to take care of.

Stewart remained behind and stared at Tootie. "I know you from somewhere, but I can't figure out where. Your dark hair is trying to trigger a memory somehow in me. Why did you say that I was on your list?"He asked looking a little shocked and confused.

"We probably know each other from a fast food place or maybe the supermarket." She said trying to avoid the truth. We may have sat in booths near each other or bumped into each other in an elevator. I bump into people all of the time that I have to figure out where I know them from."She replied sitting back down at her desk.

"No, you know me. Why am I on your list?" he asked.

"You are on a ninety day trial which is sort of a list . . .! Now, get out of my office. I have phone calls to return. Thanks for the hat" she replied and quickly picked up a phone and put it to her ear and started dialing a number, any number. She couldn't foul up their operation by digging up old bones and getting in to it with Stewart. He was working out and they needed his hands on a steering wheel.

Stewart left scratching his head looking really serious.

CHAPTER
TWENTY-ONE

The Apology

Three months flew by. Stewart slipped in and out in the mornings apparently forgetting the hat day conversation. She tried to have her back to him when he was clocking in and out. She had mixed emotions concerning him. For one thing, he looked a little like William. He had that Jewish look that she so loved about William. Her friend, Mrs. Rosamond, thought Stewart walked on water and was one of the nicest humans that she had even known. Tootie was uneasy in his presence because she remembered the names he had called her once upon a time. You don't forget being called freak and tattoo trash.

During his ninety days of employment, he had been a model employee and behaved himself. He hadn't been rude to her or any of their customers and he had started to seem like part of the business. James indicated that he felt they should keep him on permanently. She just hoped he would not remember her or their encounter in the loan department at the bank. Money to buy a home was her only goal. She was a survivor and would tolerate whatever she had to in order to become and have what she wanted. She just wanted to do her job, make the company successful, collect her yearly share of the profits, and buy herself a home. She needed to stay focused and not cause their company to take a step backwards.

It was payday. Stewart opened the office door about five thirty and entered having completed his deliveries.

"Your check is on the desk!" Tootie stated with her back to Stewart. She was trying to have as little eye contact with him as possible. She tried to be on the phone when he clocked in and out or when he came for his paycheck to avoid having to hold a conversation with him. She didn't hear him open the door and leave, so she spun around in her chair to face the inevitable.

"Is there something wrong with your check?" she asked putting the phone down and noticing for the first time what amazingly beautiful dark eyes he had behind his gold rimmed glasses. She questioned herself how she had missed seeing that. She was a wee bit attracted to him, but she was sure that was because he looked like her William.

"James says that my ninety days is up and that I have a permanent job with you. In spite of having always working in an office, I find the freedom of this job rally appealing. Traveling to a new location with every load isn't like being tied to a desk all day and sometimes missing lunch. I would like to stay here and continue to truck with James and maybe help you in the office occasionally. However, I think that you and I might have unresolved issues between us.

"I have no issues with you, Stewart. Whatever you think is a problem, take it up with James. I run the office. All employees answer to him."

"Why have you let me work here considering the way I treated you when you came to me for a loan at the bank? I have finally figured out who you are. You are the tattoo woman that I treated so badly and got fired over. Where did your tattoos go?"

"I am not interested in the past, only in what is best for this company and what puts money in my pocket. We needed a driver and you were two willing hands for a steering wheel."She replied rising from her chair feeling a bit intimidated. He was in her face.

"Why would you even consider hiring me? Are you playing some game with me?"

"I have survived very nicely without the nine thousand dollar loan that I asked you for. I have no agenda with you other than to use your hands on the steering wheel of our truck to make me money." She replied. "The office is off limits to you and I am busy. Go speak with James if you have a problem. You answer to him, not me."

"I am sorry for all the nasty things I said to you back then." He stated red faced. However, your dig about me being a thief got me fired. I hate you for that."

"Well, we are even! I hate you and you hate me. That is fair."She replied."I can live with it, if you can."

"You destroyed my hard worked for image as a banker. If you were a man, I would kick your ass." He replied angrily."You caused me to lose everything I had."

"Kick away if you think you are big enough. You are blaming me for over extending yourself and living beyond your means back then. You lost everything because you had been busy spending instead of saving. A man with money in the bank doesn't lose everything he has in a moment of unexpected disaster. I had three hundred dollars when you turned me down and I made it last till something besides your bank loan came through. Look at yourself before you blame me. I am a success who has crawled up out of a disastrous life that was forced on me. I had no parents or rich uncle to stick a silver spoon and an office job down my throat. The person you were back there was an image someone else created. I bet that you have never accomplished anything that you chose and had to pay for."

"Well, I passed the CDL test on my own and paid for the test out of my wages. Does that count in your book? I have also put a hundred dollars in your pocket and made myself a pay check with my hands on your steering wheel. Does that count? I am a survivor and one day I will have a home in the suburbs while you sit here and rot in this two room shack with your disgust for me. I know how to make money. I was a banker. I have just needed a reason to tackle life again. I owe Mrs. Rosamond for getting me this job. She will always own a piece of my heart and will be held dear in my memories. You, I will survive, leave in my dust, and never give you a second thought."He replied in an angry voice.

"I may live in a two room shack, but I know who I am and how I got here. I am the survivor. I graduated college and have become a business owner without you and your loan. Also, I won't fire you. I want you to show your true colors and be a wimpy, little, run home to Mrs. Rosamond quitter."

"You knew it was me from the first day," he retorted."I will not fail as your employee or be your hands on a wheel forever. I just might make it my goal to buy out your partner's share. Wouldn't that burn your ass, my being your equal?"

"Yes, I knew it was you and I have smiled everyday knowing that I have you under my thumb you piece of crap." She stated lying. The truth was that she was trying to keep her identity hidden. She had one goal, to buy herself a home in the suburbs and let the world that had treated her so bad pass on by.

"I apologize for the day I called you names in the bank. However, I feel sorry for you. You are jealous of anyone who has a family and a normal life. "Yes, my mother and uncle paid for my education. That doesn't make me a bad person. However, I was young and didn't appreciate their investment in me till now. Someday, I will give my children the best that I can give them and pray that they don't have a disastrous run in with someone like you. If I was guessing, you are welfare trash who had to quit school when she was sixteen because her parents were living in a car or dead from drugs leaving her suddenly to fend for herself. You hate anyone that has parents or lives a normal life."

"I think we have said it all," she replied red faced and about to explode. He had pushed all of her buttons

"We have our feelings out in the open. That is good."He replied.

"I think we understand that we hate each other. Now leave my office."

"Not before I finish my apology. I am a man of principles whether you believe it or not." He said taking a deep breath." I was up for the bank presidency. On that disastrous day we encountered each other, I had been told by Ward's secretary, who was trying to brown nose me, that a fake loan application would be crossing my desk. It was Ward's last day and he was taking one last look at me before announcing that I would be the new president. I knew he was watching and I decided to put on a show and throw you out as a bit of humor to end his career on. I thought you were a plant. Being young and stupid, I saw it as a game. I even winked at the security camera once. I didn't know your application was the real thing till he chewed my ass out over you and fired me. I am sorry for the degrading remarks I made."

"I would like to believe you, Stewart. However, as you have so nicely pointed out, I am a street kid and know that people will lie out their yang-yang if they think there is something in it for them. You stay out of my way and I will stay out of yours. You answer to James, not me."

"I was hoping that we might bury the hatchet." He replied."I am also thinking of going home and burying the hatchet with my uncle. It is me not speaking with him, not him with me. I ran into the receptionist at the bank and she said that my uncle and his wife had purposely wanted a small wedding and planned it with only the bride's mother in attendance. I am going to try to look over my not being invited. I think you might like my Uncle Ward if you ever met him. I intend to apologize to him for my childish behavior that day. I have done some growing up in the last year."

"This might surprise you, I do know Ward. We had coffee one in the shop that you and I have spoke about once upon a time. I know that he is diabetic, overweight, and a piece of crap like you."

"How do you know Ward?" he asked in shock hearing her tell personal things about his uncle.

"I know him. Did you ever stop to think that I was his lover and a last day test to see how you would handle the situation? My tattoos were false. You don't see them now do you? You screwed me over as a pretend applicant and I don't think he took too kindly to it. Am I wrong? "She asked smugly stretching the truth to get to him.

'Oh shit!" he replied. "No wonder he was so irate with me."

About that time, James walked in and saw the two in each other's faces. He was going to ask Stewart to help him jump his pickup. The battery was dead. However, it looked like he was going to have to referee an all out mouthing war.

"I gather you two are having a friendly word or two. Should I come back?" he asked eyeing Tootie who was red faced.

"I just asked Tootie to join me for dinner tonight at the fast food place down the street which is in my budget. She has found my dinner invitation low class and insulting." Stewart stated as he stared Tootie in the eye.

"We are lowly garbage dumpster men with no hope of ever having a meaningful relationship with a woman of higher social status. Now, you are just like me, a Tootie reject."

"Tell me, Tootie; am I just a garbage man? Let James hear your opinion of me as well as your turn down."

"You are two hands on the company's truck steering wheel. Now, you are an idiot who has stuck his foot in his mouth who is going to spend some of his hard earned cash feeding me tonight. You asked. I accept. I do hope that you know what a fork is and that you don't burp after dessert."

"I do hope you dress appropriately. I would hate to have my friends think that I was dating a woman with no taste. A woman wearing men's driving boots and a squirrel skin cap isn't exactly sexy or attractive."

"Should I dress appropriately and sexy, you wouldn't be able to keep your hands or eyes off of me. I think I will wear my boots and hat for safety reasons. I just imagine that you are a pervert that I might have to slap upside the head."

"Should a pervert try to assault you while in my company, I will tell him to go ahead. You are a dried up aging old maid who hasn't had a man to make love to her in years. I would be doing you a favor."

"What have the two of you been drinking, wacky juice?" James asked interrupting their war of words. "Do the two of you want to tell me what is going on?"

"I really appreciate your hiring me and being my friend. However, Tootie and I hate each other. I won't be back on Monday. I have my reasons."

"Come on Stewart. Whatever is wrong between you and Tootie can be worked out. She is a high strung female who is probably having one of those chocolate bar days. Look over her. Women don't always make rational decisions or think straight like a man does. They are emotional crazies at certain times of the month. I need you."

"High strung, emotional, and a crazy, huh?" questioned Tootie slowly repeating what James had said letting his words sink in to her core."You just chose to belittle me in front of a ninety day hire in. I am your business partner who has poured her soul as well as her knowledge as a business major into this business making it successful. I am smarter than you or Stewart ever thought about being. He is a piece of banking reject trash and you are a high school dropout! I will start a new business from scratch and you are now on your own. I quit! We will come to an agreement on Monday and split the company assets. This lot and shack are mine. You can have the cash and Stewart."

"Come on, Tootie. I didn't mean what I said about women. I just didn't want Stewart walking. We need him." James begged.

Tootie entered the back room which was now her bedroom and slammed the door.

"I am really sorry, James. I didn't intend to cause trouble between you and Tootie. I will look for work elsewhere. She will cool down with me gone."

"You are not leaving. I need you. We will buy her flowers or something on Monday."

"Personally, "stated Stewart biting his lip. "I know she means what she says. I have battled words with her before. She is a force to deal with."

CHAPTER
TWENTY-TWO

Starting Over

Friday night was the ending of another portion of Tattootie Tootie Beecham's life journey. Her world was suddenly upside down and she was facing reinventing herself once more. She didn't sleep well because she dreamed of marrying Ward and having butterball children. On waking just before midnight, the dream irritated her and she got up to get a drink. She had worked hard to stuff her memories of him way down deep where they didn't hurt. Fighting with Stewart had caused her nightmare to become fresh and painful again. He opened up a bottomless pit inside her where she stuffed everything that hurt her. Now Ward had climbed out of the pit and was alive seducing her in her dreams. While drinking that Friday night late glass of water, she decided the problem was she hadn't taken the time to grieve. She needed to go back to where they met, leave a flower on the table, and bury him once and for all as if he were a dead man. It was time to face her nightmare before she began a new life.

Saturday morning, Tootie rose early and went to the bank. She had a freeze put on the business account money. James had been good to her. However, she knew that he had spent his share of the profits and was living paycheck to paycheck till they once more split the profits for the year. He was not a person who saved for a rainy day or planned for the future. She had to watch out for her interests. No one else was going to. After putting a hold on their business account, she called a woman attorney that she knew and hired her to recover her half of the dumpster business in a fair split. She asked for the commercial lot and shack and offered James the cash in the business account. The two room shack was the only home she had and she wasn't budging from it, if she could help it.

After a visit to the attorney downtown, she checked into the Biltmore for a couple nights with plans to walk to the coffee shop mid morning and bury Ward.

"She had a reason for wanting to keep the lot in the industrial park. It was next door to Mrs. Rosamond, the only friend that she had. She just couldn't go off and leave her there alone. She was sure that Stewart would eventually abandon her when he got enough money to rent an apartment and move on. Mrs. Rosamond and William were all she had. Mrs. Rosamond had become like a mother to her.

Rising early Saturday morning before the crack of dawn, in order to miss any further confrontation with Stewart and James, Tattootie threw an overnight bag in her car trunk and headed downtown. Two years ago, she had walked to the bank trying to save bus fare. Now, she had a car and it paid for. Also, she had forty some thousand of her own money deposited in a bank in the industrial park area. She had her college degree as well as a CDL having graduated trucking school. Now it was time to reinvent her twenty-three year old self again.

After checking into the Biltmore, she walked downtown to confront her memories of Ward. The walk was pleasant. It was the first week in April and the sunshine felt wonderful on her face. She recalled what luxury sunshine was when she was living on top of the laundry building with only a plastic shower curtain she had found for a tent. She was proud of her successes and suddenly a feeling of being someone swept over her. She had accomplished her goals. Now it was time to set new ones and move forward never looking back after today. As she passed the bench that her and Ward had sat on, she smiled. Her bench was still hers and so was her future. She had survived very nicely without him and was now somebody. Today she was burying her past and Ward. She had made up her mind to never return after these two days at the Biltmore.

CHAPTER
TWENTY-THREE

Confrontation with Ward

Friday night in her anger, she had forgotten to eat. She also had failed to eat breakfast. Her stomach was growling. So, she decided to drop in at the coffee shop to have a bite to eat. She would return and sit on the bus bench later. The coffee shop had been freshly painted outside. She could remember exactly what it looked like the day Ward took her there for coffee. She had mixed emotions and felt a little teary eyed. She told herself that it was okay to cry when you put someone you loved in the ground. This was no different.

A stranger in a grey business suit opened the door for her. As she entered, she noticed that he had tears in his eyes. She watched as he headed toward the back and the hallway that led to the men's rest room. As a rule, little boys are conditioned that men don't cry. She wondered what had reduced him to tears. She felt for him. There had been many times that she had cried alone. She had never had a friend to share her sorrows with. Her thoughts were interrupted when a waitress spoke to her.

"The only table available is back there by the window. You had better grab it quick. The lunch hour pencil pushers are about to descend on us."

"Thank you for the insight." She replied and then had a moment of empathy for the man who was crying."There is a man in a gray suit that has just entered the male's rest room. I know there isn't another small booth or table left. You may seat him with me if he is willing. I think he might need a friend."

"I saw him. He was crying, wasn't he?" the waitress replied.

"Yes! I know what it is like to cry alone."

"I will keep an eye out for him." She replied handing Tootie a menu and pointing her towards the back.

The coffee shop was packed to overflowing. Tootie ignored the crowd and made her way to the tiny table for two along the back wall. She sat down after removing her lightweight pink jacket. She didn't go out very often. Today was a special occasion, the beginning of a new journey into the business world. After checking into the Biltmore Inn, she had taken the time to put on her makeup and dress up for the day. She had worn nothing but jeans, T-shirts, driver's boots, and ball caps for the last year or so. It felt good to feel like a woman and have on feminine things. She really felt sexy and good about herself wearing the black stockings and heels she had saved for a special occasion. Something in her told her that today was a major turning point on her life path. She was excited and letting her brain run away with new ideas for the future.

As she sat there, she eyed the booth where she and Ward had sat. Time had not erased the pain of his not calling. She remembered her tears when after two weeks she realized he was not the friend that he projected himself to be. She had trusted him and told him things she wouldn't have told anyone. She really thought that the two of them had made a connection. Her naïve, fragile ego felt like it had been raped back then. She remembered all the tears and then shutting down and freezing her heart. The empathy for the man crying was the first time she had felt anything for another human since then.

A waitress interrupted her thoughts as she was staring out the window into a small garden terrace about six feet wide running between the coffee shop and another building. There were trellises with growing vines and wild grasses. She wanted a place like that when she got her home in the suburbs. She wanted a peaceful place with a little table and two chairs where she could go out in private and have her morning coffee.

"May I sit this gentleman with you? I am short on tables and I assume you are here alone."

Tootie looked up and was shocked to see Ward standing behind the waitress grinning.

"I am sorry, but I am here with someone. He is in the men's room. How are you Ward?" she asked politely and was extremely glad that she had the stranger to claim as her table companion.

"I will sit at the counter, Millie. Save me a place!" He said to the waitress and then turned to Tootie. "I am fine, thank you. Why haven't you called?"

"It is my personal opinion that it is a man's place to make the first call." She retorted not smiling.

"I honestly lost your number, Tootie. The Tattoo parlor refuses to give me a number for you. I have begged and even offered them money."

"I saw your wedding announcement in the paper. Your attempts to contact me at the Tattoo parlor only says one thing, you see me as some cheap piece of white trash that you can play around on your wife with. I have standards and they don't include a man who would play around on his wife or seek out a cheap thrill with a white trash girl on his last day of being single. I don't know what your game was back then, Ward. However, I don't play games. You are a married man who should be ashamed of himself. If you will excuse me, I have moved on and am here with someone."

"I honestly lost your number, Tootie and I can explain my marriage. Let me call you and we will discuss it."

"I am sorry Ward. There comes my gentleman friend now." She replied seeing the first waitress escorting the gray suited gentleman her way.

Ward looked up at the man heading their way. Suddenly, he got the strangest open mouthed look on his face. Then he quickly left not saying another word. He took a stool on the far end of the counter facing her table. She purposely ignored him. She was burying him today. She would never be any married man's mistress. Her eyes started to fill with tears. She turned toward the window to hide them.

CHAPTER
TWENTY-FOUR

William's Tears

"I told this gentleman that you were willing to share your table." The first waitress stated pointing the man in the gray suit to the chair across the table from her.

"Thank you for sharing your table. Do I know you?" he asked opening up his menu still visibly teary eyed.

"You opened the door for me when we entered. I was given the last table, so I asked the waitress to tell you that I would share it with you if you weren't meeting someone."

"I guess the kindnesses we show do return to us. I need a little Karmic return." He stated.

Tootie smiled and looked him over. She knew that Ward was watching and she wanted to appear interested in her lunch companion, even if he was a stranger. She knew the teary eyed man from somewhere. She searched her memory for the answer as she admired his wonderful Jewish facial features and black hair. Ward had some of the same Jewish look. She told herself that the two could be distant relatives of some sort because they looked somewhat alike.

"I am a firm believer in Karma. I try to not do anything that might come back and bite me in the butt." She replied. "My name is Tootie. "

"My name is William. I am afraid I will not be a very pleasant lunch companion. I have been out at Mt. Olive Cemetery trying to say goodbye to someone I love." He stated glancing teary eyed at her over the menu.

Jo Hammers

"I am sorry. Was someone near and dear to you buried this morning?" she asked and suddenly realized he was the four o'clock shadow man from years before. He was her William. She remembered is billfold and the snapshot he showed her of his children and wife.

"Their deaths took place a year ago today." He replied not going in to details."I live above the coffee shop in one of the studio apartments. Today is an extremely bad memory day for me. All of my family died one year ago today. I have come in here because I need to be with people even if they are strangers. My grief, and the depression accompanying it, has just about destroyed me. I don't trust myself to be alone today. Thank you for sharing your table."

The waitress came and quickly, took their orders, and poured them some coffee. Then she hurried away leaving them to their conversation.

"I had coffee here with a man I naively pictured myself marrying. The relationship died. This coffee shop is the cemetery that I am visiting. Like you, I am laying him and our relationship to rest and grieving." She replied and then halfway wondered if William sitting across from her was real. She had loved the imaginary William so long, she wasn't sure that they weren't one and the same."

"We are a teary eyed pair, aren't we?" He retorted looking in to her wet eyes.

"Would you like to tell me about the deaths in your family? Sometimes it is easier to tell strangers what we are feeling because they have no expectations from us." she replied as she sipped her coffee and imagined him sitting there clothed only in one of her pink bath towels.

"You don't know who I am, do you?" he asked looking seriously at her.

"No, I'm sorry I don't!" she replied putting cream and sugar in her coffee.

"My wife shot and killed our four children a year ago today. She killed them first and then waited for me to come home from the office and shot me as I stepped from my car in the driveway. Neighbors pulling in their drives heard the shots and saw me slump to the ground. Then they watched in horror as she turned the revolver to her own head and discharged it. Inside the house she had sat my children up on stools at the breakfast bar with bowls of cereal in front of them. While they were eating, she circled around behind them and shot them all in the back starting with the oldest. She left them all day slumped over their cereal bowls. The newspapers and television stations went wild with the story. A year has passed, but my nightmares and grief haven't lessened. I am not handling it very well."

90

"I share your grief, William. My parents committed a double suicide when I was three. When the first gunshot sounded, I ran and crawled under a bed. Being three, the loud sound frightened me. What I recall is my mother yelling for me to come to her just before she put a bullet thru her head. My hiding was not a snag that she had planned on. She didn't have time to look for me because neighbors were beating on the door. She shot herself and slumped down on top of my father who was holding my favorite stuffed animal. I think I was in his arms when he went down. I am a survivor of suicidal parents who intended to take me with them, but failed."

"We do share a common nightmare." He stated reaching over and putting his hand on top of hers in a comforting gesture and then quickly removed it."My wife and I had a perfect marriage, or so I thought. We volunteered in the community as well as attended synagogue. The boys played soccer and my twin little girls were just little cuties who were in to fashion dolls. We had everything going for us. I thought we were living the American Dream."

"My parents were both members of a church. My dad was a deacon and my mother a Sunday school teacher. They seemed normal, or so I am told. I was three and don't remember too much about them other than running from the sound and the shock of being dropped from my father's arms."

"Status was everything to my wife, Betty. She was intent upon climbing the social ladder. I was the manager of a bank and up for promotion. The position of bank president was up for grabs and she wanted to be known as a banker's wife. I didn't get the promotion and she asked me for a divorce saying she didn't want to be married to a loser. I did not want the divorce and begged her to stay with me for the children's sakes. She laughed in my face and yelled that she didn't want me or them."

"It sounds as though we have both had a deep dark pit of relationship rejection to climb out of."

"It gets worse. She confessed to me that she was going to marry my cousin, Ward, who is a multimillionaire. She said they were going to fly away and start a new life in France. "He stated wiping wet eyes on a table napkin. "I couldn't give her what she wanted, so she chose a new prey, my cousin. However, he wasn't agreeable to her advances and taped her on security cameras. He immediately called me and showed me the tape. I didn't believe him at first. I stormed out of his office, told him to go to hell, and quit."

"I am sorry William. Betrayal is like a knife that sticks you in your gut over and over."

She honestly thought that she was going to marry my wealthy cousin and go her happy way discarding me and our children like we were garbage. "

"I wish I had known you, I would have been there for you." She replied with big solemn eyes.

"She flew home from France when her money played out and she realized my cousin wasn't going to meet her there with his millions. I was a fool and gave into her pleas to reconcile. She stayed one night in my arms. I have never loved anyone but her and I wanted her back. She just wanted entrance into my house and the opportunity to take me and the children out with her. I could have prevented it. I was a fool and let her in!"

"When someone intends to do something violent, there is no stopping them. If it hadn't been that day, it would have been another. She would have found a way to make it happen. You can't blame yourself, William. You are a loving man and you made good choices. Reconciliation is a good thing where two people love each other. You acted out of love."

"I am well known around the city due to my job and the fact I have done a lot of charity volunteer work. The whole sordid affair has been front line news and I can't escape from it. My cousin, Ward's reputation has been damaged somewhat by it. He isn't speaking to me at the moment. I thought for awhile that he was having an affair with her. I went off the deep end and accused him of it. My whole life ended. I don't know how to get it back."

"You have a cousin named Ward?" she asked taken back a bit.

"Yes. He is sitting at the end of the counter. He is the one wearing the dark suit. He is a magnet for women. In spite of the fact he was married, my Betty wanted him and called from France trying to get him to dump his new wife and marry her. He has a way with women. I was a blind fool not seeing that my Betty was attracted to him."

"When did your nightmare begin?" She asked in shock hearing a whole tragedy that was taking place while she was trying to get over her own victimization.

"The day my nightmare started, Ward was retiring and had tickets to go to Hawaii. He married the next morning his secretary. Now that one surprised me. I have never known Ward to date anyone low class. He always has a socialite somewhere on his arm at charity events. He was along with my Betty late afternoon before the day of his wedding and she declared her love for him. I don't understand why the two of them were alone in the back of the bank building and why he chose to show me the security tape of them. I would have been happier not knowing and my wife and children might be alive. He set a whole chain of events rolling that destroyed my marriage and resulted in the deaths of my children. I would have forgiven her for an affair, even with him. "

"I see." Tootie stated with a knife in her gut. Apparently, Ward had left her and returned to the bank and played some game with his wife. She tried to not show her emotions. She was there to bury Ward and this stranger was helping her do it. She was appalled that Ward had moved from her to another woman that day she had tried so hard to forget. "So how have you been supporting yourself since then? Have you returned to the job that you had?"

"I quit my position as bank manager and haven't asked to be rehired. To be truthful, I would like to go where no one knows me, far- far- far away. I feel like all my friends, family, and acquaintances are judging me for what Betty did. I can't face them. I have been living off of my savings."

"Running away won't help, William. I ran from my foster care home at sixteen to forget, but the memories always haunt you. The best you can do is live well and stay clear of the crazies who want to torment you. Do you know what a tattoo model is?"

"I suppose it would be like any model. They would model Tattoo designs."

"That is how I made my living after I ran away from foster care. Tattoo artists would draw their designs on my skin with ordinary ball point pens in blue, red, and green. They looked like real tattoos but they would wash off in about ten days or so. I was paid well for it and I worked my way thru high school and college at that vocation. The tattoos looked real and people ostracized, poked fun at me, and called me a freak seeing my body covered with them. I was young and couldn't find employment. I survived in spite of all the stares and rude comments from humans that society called normal. I was the normal one. I had a goal to go to college and be someone. I had no family or extended family to turn to. I was all alone just as you are now. Survive, William. Reinvent yourself into a new you and build yourself a new life."

"I am alone. I don't want to be alone. What good is reinventing me if I have no one to share my life with?"

"Both of our families are dead; we can't help that. We can grieve, but that is all we can do. One day I chose to walk away from the foster care hell that I lived in. When I hit the streets, I had nothing and no one to turn to. What I did have was a dream. Your family's tragic deaths are like my foster care hell. They have you in bondage. You need to walk away and set yourself a goal and walk towards it. You don't need friends, family, or acquaintances that make snide remarks and faces concerning your unfortunate circumstances. Today is the day that you must decide that you want more than what life has dished out to you. I made it and so can you. I am college educated, own my own business, and I am working on my masters degree. I am alone in the world, just as you are. If you wish, I will be your friend. The universe has chosen to let our paths cross today."

"You don't know how much your words mean to me. Could I buy you dinner tonight?" He asked. "I think I want you to tell me more about reinventing myself. I need direction."

"I will try to point you in a new direction if you will help me with ideas to reorganize my business. There are no free rides in this life. I am willing to be your friend if you are willing to make it a two way street." She replied.

"Be my friend, Tootie and be patient with me. I know that I have got to lay my family to rest. I tried to say goodbye to them today. I couldn't do it. Help me!"

"I think I have plans for you William. How would you feel about moving to the industrial district on the other side of town?"

"That might work for me. I don't know anyone over there."

"I accept your dinner invitation and you as a gift from the universe. I need a friend and you need a friend. I am a strong, successful business woman and a survivor of what life has thrown at me. I have chosen not to date and concentrate on becoming successful. However, I am tired of being alone. I think you are too. I don't have a lot of time to waste doing a song and dance with you. I have three days till it is back to the grindstone for me. Would you like to go and be a part of my world? I will be your friend as well as create a position for you in my business."

"You don't realize how much I need a friend." He stated eyeing her."Let us make the most of your three days and yes I will go with you. I have nothing here to hold on to."

As he sat looking at her, he realized how utterly beautiful she was. She was not a prim and proper beauty like Betty. She was a gorgeous raven haired successful young woman with a gentle side to her that no one saw. He could see himself falling madly in love with her. Had the universe taken Betty from him so that Tootie could come? He was ashamed of his thought. He felt strange as he looked into Tootie's eyes. He saw a woman that he wanted and she wasn't Betty.

"I hope you don't mind if we discuss a little business at dinner. I need someone to bounce a few business ideas off of. I am staying at the Biltmore in room 203. Is seven okay? "

"Seven it is. Do you mind riding in a pickup? I sold the family car to help pay for Hospital bills."

"You are going to be surprised at the vehicle I drive!" She replied amused. She was going to love taking him one night to dinner in her dumpster delivery truck.

"You have a mysterious side. I like intrigue. How do you feel about a man who loves to cook?"

"I work twelve to sixteen hours every day and am lucky to catch a fast food hamburger on the run. You are the first person I have taken time to have lunch with in way over a year. Does that tell you anything? Perhaps you can save me from fast food madness!" she stated laughing.

"Next weekend, I will fix you the finest brunch you have ever eaten? Do you like quiche?"

"William, I love quiche. How would you feel about growing old with a round little woman that you have fattened up like a pig?"

"They say a large woman will keep you warm on a long, cold winter night. I am a skinny little man with big cold feet who needs a back to warm them on."He stated laughing. "I think I will nickname you my little Oink!"

"How does Cold Foot sound for you?"She retorted laughing.

"I have an appointment that I can't get out of. I must say goodbye until this evening. You don't know how bad it is hurts me to go off and leave you sitting here. Now that I have found you, I am going to be paranoid about losing you. However, I have a doctor's appointment."

As far as I am concerned, William, we have a whole lifetime ahead of us to be together. I am a one man woman and I have just chosen you. Do what you need to do and pick me up at seven. Bring your suitcase and your photos of your family and Betty. Having her photo on your night stand is alright with me. I understand. You won't be returning here, because I don't have time for the dating game."

"You are going to tell me what to do and when to do it, aren't you?" he stated laughing.

Jo Hammers

"I am a no non-sense woman who knows what she wants. You will live, love, and die in my arms when we are old." She replied.

I want to start our relationship being honest. My family's deaths have just about destroyed me. I was seriously thinking of ending it all when I walked in here this morning."

Tootie quickly reached over and put her hand on top of his and gave it a gentle squeeze."Do not die William! I need you!"

Tears rolled down his cheeks. "I need you too!"

CHAPTER
TWENTY-FIVE

Pink Towels

William Goldman stood outside Tootie's door at the Biltmore Inn and took a deep breath. He wanted to knock. At the same time, he felt like he was being a traitor to his family. How could he think about loving anyone but them? He didn't know how to answer that question. He was a family man and had sworn to love Betty thru eternity. His children were his world. His family was his life. Now they were gone and he was starting from square one. He didn't know how to let them go. He didn't know how to love someone new.

What he did know was that he wanted to fall into Tootie's arms for comfort and safety. He needed her. At the same time, he felt like a cheating husband. His children would never understand him loving anyone but their mother. However, he had dreamed about Tootie for several years. His Jewish God must have seen his coming loss and prepared her for him. He needed her. He knew he needed her.

At the same time, he felt so guilty. If Betty and the children were alive, he was an honorable man and would choose them. That made him feel equally as guilty. He wasn't giving this new woman that God had sent him a fair shake. He took another deep breath to calm his jittery nerves.

At seven on the dot, William knocked on Tootie's door at the Biltmore Inn. She quickly opened the door and let him in. His heart skipped a beat. She had on a black cocktail dress with black leggings. The dead man in him suddenly came alive. He knew that he was going to fall madly in love with her. However, he didn't feel that he had the right to. He was thrilled to see her, but his stomach was in knots due to his memories.

"Whoa, turn around and let me look at you. I will have to beat the wolves off of you tonight. You are eye candy." He stated grinning.

"Will you feel that way when I am round from eating your cooking next year?" she shot back spinning around for him. She was used to doing the modeling bit from the tattoo days.

"I will have to fatten you up so the wolves won't know how gorgeous you are. I never plan on losing you. I have hit the jackpot." He laughed.

"Well then, quit staring and help me with my coat. I think you have promised me dinner."

"Right now, food is the last thing on my mind." He shot back. "Do I really belong to you?"

"I claimed you today, didn't I? I hope you have your suitcase down in your truck. You will look funny sleeping in my lingerie. I like a man in pajamas. However, if I have to take you wearing my little black gown, I am not picky. I will take you as a cross dresser."

William stepped over to her and took her in his arms and kissed her gently and then passionately like he had never been loved. He ran his hands all over her and she did the same. They didn't make it to dinner. They found what was missing in both of their lives. It was like they had come home to each other after a long, long separation. After a couple of hours making love, William held Tootie close in his arms with his head nestled on top of her head.

"You are the other half of me, aren't you?' he asked.

"No, you are the other half of me," she replied.

"I think I am ready, Tootie to lay Betty to rest. Making love to you has opened my eyes to what two people can be together. You wanted me! You made love to me. I have never had that experience. Forgive me for talking about Betty, but I always want to be honest with you. From the day I married her, it was me on top of her. She would just lay there letting me do my thing. She never once made love to me."

"You are the man that I have chosen to be in my bed and I have every intention of finding pleasure making love to you. I have always known what I have wanted out of life. When you sat down at my table this morning, I knew instantly I wanted you."

"I am one lucky man. Now that I have had you, I never want to be apart from you. You lead in life and I will follow. Whatever you want, I will support your efforts." He stated kissing the top of her head and holding her nude body to him tightly. "You are my new beginning. God has smiled on me in my pit of bitter despair."

"You promised me dinner." She stated as he held her.

"We are in to fine dining tonight. We are ordering in Pizza and flip a coin to see which one of us gets dressed to answer the door." He laughed snuggling her.

"We are going to have a lot of pizza nights aren't we?" she asked laughing.

"I think we are setting our first family tradition. After we make love, we will flip a coin and then eat pizza." He stated laughing.

"I have never had a family, William. "This is a first for me. You will probably never understand how important you are to me as well as what this night means to me. You will be my pink towel man. I know what I want out of life. You are it and I am going to take very good care of you in every way possible."

"You are going to be the man in our family and I am going to be the housewife, aren't I?" he asked grinning and holding her securely in his arms.

"You've got it. If we should ever have children, you are doing the diapering and the nurturing. I will be the bread winner and you can run away every night into my arms. Think of me and my arms as your hiding place. You don't have to think of me as a wife, William. I am willing for you to love me in a different way that is right for us. I am not a stereotype woman."

"I am one lucky man to have found you." He replied nuzzling his face next to hers."Is it alright if I use your pink towels? I can see myself wrapped in one watching you get ready for work in the morning."

"I wouldn't have you any other way."

CHAPTER
TWENTY-SIX

An Ending is Just a New Beginning

Tootie took her share of the dumpster company's assets and started a trucking company called HI-HEELS TRUCKING. She hired only women drivers with the exception of James her old business partner who applied when his dumpster business bellied up. She put her savings down on five trucks and ten trailers that had been repossessed by a loan company. Her hands manned the steering wheel of the first truck till her business got started. In the next three years she kept expanding till she had a fleet of fifty semis and sixty employees. She made herself and fragile William an excellent living. With time, his grief lessened. Together, they tore down their two room shack of an office and built Tootie's dream home on the company's ground.

Mrs. Rosamond surprised everyone with announcing that she was going to remarry about a year after William and Tootie became a couple. Tootie was the maid of honor at her shocking wedding and William was the best man. Stewart in his mid twenties married Mrs. Rosamond. It had to be love, because she had no money or assets. The kind old lady told Tootie that he had accidently seen her butterfly and that he was a mad man after that pursuing her.

Tootie accepted her friends and employees just the way they were. She even buried the hatchet with Stewart after he married her friend. Remembering what a hard time she had trying to survive, she looked for and hired women with goals who weren't normal. Every employee she had respected her and was thankful for their jobs to feed themselves. William walked away from the suburbs leaving no forwarding address and abandoning all together who he once was. He married Tootie and took her name becoming Mr. Tootie Beecham. He lived quietly with Tootie in seclusion and kept her pink bathroom towels always washed and fresh on the bathroom rods. His Jewish God had sent her to save him. He was sure of that. The book of Joel in his Old Testament said that old men would dream dreams. He had dreamed of her, her pink towels, and inked body when she was Tattootie. She had made her way to him when he was at his lowest moment of despair. God had let them find each other. After his grief lessened, he started studies to be a Rabbi. Tootie supported him in his goal.

Stewart Goldman was shocked to death when William came to live beyond the tracks of the city and married Tootie. The two of them embraced, cried, and became the best of pals for the rest of their lives. They were family. Stewart remodeled Mrs. Rosamond's living room into a gypsy's reading room and he took up the Tarot Cards and also did crystal ball readings. Together they lived comfortably and Stewart became famous as a reader. Mrs. Rosamond had fed him, loved him, and taught him to be special and wear a coat of many colors.

No one knew what happened to Ward Goldman. After he divorced Madge Burns, he closed the doors on the bank. There was no one to hand the presidency down to and he decided to walk away. He had made his fortune and in doing so had lost himself and the woman he knew he was meant to be with. About a year after closing the bank, a book hit the best seller list titled 'DON'T LOSE HER NUMBER, YOU WILL BE SORRY' By Ward Goldman.

Also Available by Jo Hammers...

Coffins & Cadavers

The Joel Manuscript

Zook's Place

Made in the USA
Monee, IL
10 February 2021